Do You Know
The Ave Maria Violin?

Yoshiko Kagawa

Based on the true historical events

Contents

Main Characters

Asuka: A fourteen-year-old Japanese girl who lives in Tokushima, Japan, and has been studying the violin since childhood.

Mr. Kiyohara: A music shop owner who introduces Asuka to the Ave Maria Violin.

Mr. Calsas: A resident musician in Poland who tells Asuka about the history of the Ave Maria Violin.

Hannah: A fourteen-year-old Jewish girl to whom the Ave Maria Violin first belonged.

Klaus Berger: A German musician who followed Hannah's family to Auschwitz.

Arles: A Jewish musician who conducted the prison orchestra at Auschwitz.

Leo: A Polish cellist who played in the prisoner orchestra at Auschwitz.

David: A German prisoner of war at Bando POW camp, Japan, during WWI who became a resident baker.

Paul: A German prisoner of war at Bando POW camp during WWI who crafted the Ave Maria Violin.

Prelude: My Story

I used to spend my days aimlessly.

I attended school only because that was what everyone else did. I only had a handful of friends from my neighborhood.

I did schoolwork simply because my mom would get mad at me if I didn't, so I pretended to be a good girl so as not to get grounded.

Whatever that piqued my interest then, didn't come from any burning desire from within; rather from the surroundings, under the living conditions I was in, and through the limited perspective of a fourteen-year-old.

I didn't think it was unusual. I thought it was how most kids my age felt.

I was convinced that I would go on living like this—until I came across that violin.

Chapter 1: Asuka

1

Amid the lively chatter during the five minutes recess between the homeroom and the first period, Ayumi, who sat in front of me, turned around and asked.

"Asuka, have you thought about your career path?"

Ayumi and I had been next-door neighbors all our lives, and now, in our sophomore year at junior high, we were inseparable. We liked to talk about the latest comic books and traded teen magazines, and lately, we've been busy watching her crush on the soccer field.

That morning during the homeroom, questionnaires had been handed out asking about our career interests. Ayumi held hers, giving me a serious look.

"Our career paths, huh...?"

She wasn't the only one who looked solemn. I had some ideas about what I wanted to do but was afraid that it wouldn't be easy to achieve. The hardest part would be to convince my mom. I wasn't even sure if I was serious enough to want it that much.

"Well, it would be great if I could make some money playing the violin but..."

"You mean you aren't following in your dad's footsteps?" she asked.

My dad is a doctor. Ever since I was very young, everyone seemed to assume that I would also become one someday, so much so that I just started to go along with it. But the medical profession and performing arts are completely different and, I thought, I could never be as good a doctor like my dad

"I could never succeed him! Know why? Because I want to get married by the time I'm twenty-four. From then on, I'm going to be a housewife."

"So, which one is it? A violinist or a housewife?"

"Do I have to choose just one?"

Ayumi looked rather stunned by my question and said,

"Being both a violinist and a housewife wouldn't be easy. My cousin just had a baby, and she's having a really hard time balancing her career and being a mom!"

"I suppose you're right…"

It never occurred to me that being a housewife would be all that hard. Now I wondered how playing the violin would fit into my plans. Truth be told, I hadn't given a serious thought about my future.

"Doesn't your mom want you to become a doctor? My mom seems to think so. Oh hey, speaking of you and your mom . . ." Ayumi burst into laughter. "That fight you two had yesterday was something else!" She giggled some more.

After school the day before, I decided to skip my usual violin practice and went straight next door to hang out with Ayumi. My mother came charging in when she found out, screaming my name so loud I was certain the whole block had heard.

"Asuka!" Her furious voice seemed to come from the depths of hell, and she had me so scared that I rushed home in a panic.

"It's a bigger deal for her when I skip violin practice compared to her wanting me to become a doctor. You know who really wants to be a violinist? My mom, not me."

"Your mom plays?"

"Well, no. When she was young, there was an older girl in the neighborhood who was good at it, and Mom was desperate to learn. She begged her parents to allow her to take lessons, but they were against the idea, so she never got a chance."

"So your mom's the one who likes the violin."

"Right. Still, I've been thinking lately that maybe I want to become a violinist. But if I told her I wanted to teach at the conservatory, she'd flip."

I started my piano lessons when I was two, and the violin at three. I'd been playing these instruments for well over a decade now. I could play Vitali's *Chaconne* from memory and had progressed in my lessons to the advanced intermediate level. Among the other young people who aspired to become professional musicians, I was neither ahead nor behind, maybe just average. If I were serious about becoming a violinist, I knew I needed to practice a lot harder, because there were many other kids my age who spent a lot more hours practicing than I did.

"But Asuka, everyone says you're a miracle at the violin. My mom says so, too. You got a recommendation to go and study under a teacher in Tokyo, didn't you?"

"Yeah, well, maybe I'm just a bit better compared to the kids who don't play at all, but there are millions who are just as good as me. When I was in third grade, my violin teacher did suggest that I should go to Tokyo to take lessons once a month."

I lived in the city of Tokushima on the western island of Shikoku. Tokyo seemed far away, like a city of dreams. I was delighted just to be able to go to the capital for one lesson with the teacher I'd been introduced to. But when I got there, I was overwhelmed by the high standards of the other students there and cried all the way home in defeat. Having prided myself in being regarded as a miracle in a small city, it was a devastating blow for me to see the real talents in action. That was the moment I realized that I was just mediocre. I felt ashamed for my arrogance. All of a sudden, I was experiencing a bitter dejection. What's more, I was terrified of my mother discovering that I wasn't a miracle after all.

My mother was going to take me to Tokyo again the following month, but I threw a huge tantrum and locked myself in my bedroom. Maybe she had sensed the reason for my behavior, as she didn't force me to go.

It went on like that for several months until my mother seemed to have finally given up. There was no more talk of lessons in Tokyo. It wasn't that I hated the violin, but at that time, I just wanted to play as I pleased, not as a professional soloist. Whenever I was asked about my hopes for the future, instead of saying I wanted to become a musician, I just blurted out that I wanted to get into some type of work that would allow me to play the violin. I also started to think that maybe my mother was right, that becoming a doctor might be my best option.

"I wonder if my mother would blow her top if I wrote on this survey that I wanted to get into the music school. . ."

Back when I was praised as a miracle, my mother seemed to have high hopes that her daughter might become a professional violinist. But from the time that I refused to take lessons in Tokyo with a top-rated teacher, she seemed to have given up.

The reason why she still allowed me to continue playing, I sensed, was because she wanted me to broaden my interests outside my schoolwork and later, my career. Her latest thing was to collect prospectuses from famous prep schools and cram schools and to take me on school tours, even though the high school entrance exams were more than a year away. She believed without the slightest doubt that I would eventually decide to enroll in medical school, and that I would play the violin very well as a hobby.

It's not that I wasn't at all interested in medicine. But I had yet to fully make up my mind, and her constant barrage of preparations was annoying. Mom would have been mad if I said that to her face, so I just kept my mouth shut. But the tension was always there. I often felt it between us over our different views for my future.

"Asuka, the next time you and your mother fight, don't come running to my place, or she'd get mad at me, too," Ayumi said in a teasing tone. She knew all about the daily arguments my mother and I had over my violin practice.

2

One day, a music shop owner from whom we bought my first violin contacted us about some good ones he had in stock. They say that finding your perfect violin is a matter of fate, though to be honest, the one that I was using since I was in elementary school came to me rather as a compromise. Out of the several violins that this shopkeeper had recommended, I thought the one I chose produced a pretty good tone. But when you are in competitions, there is something to be desired in the sounds it produces. Mine had a thick, bland sound like a cheap toy, although it didn't bother me back then.

My mother, who knew very little about violins, cared less about the tone than she did about the price tag, which was roughly a million yen (about $10,000). Among the top-ranked children that you would see at competitions, quite a few of them performed with the ones that cost more than ten-fold. Mom seemed to be convinced that, to perform well, I also needed an expensive instrument. The plan, therefore, was to upgrade whenever the shop restocked.

An expensive violin has excellent tone color, but I think it's also up to the player to maximize its potential to match the price tag. Just because I had a fantastic violin didn't exactly make me a brilliant player. I knew that simply getting a new violin would never get me the invites to the ranks of the top competitors unlike how my mother envisioned. Still, I was happy and excited about the idea of an upgrade. For a girl like me who lived in the boring old countryside, shopping for a new violin was a big deal.

We set foot into the shop, and a gentleman came out from behind the counter to introduce himself as Mr. Kiyohara. The shop was called Kiyohara Musical Instruments, so I figured he was the owner. It had been about three years since I last came to this shop, so I had forgotten what he looked like. He was in his mid-forties, though he looked younger, sort of like a dependable older brother type.

"I've been expecting you. You must be Miss Asuka Murakami. Let me show you, ladies, the back room."

Inside the shop were not only violins but also violas, cellos, as well as contrabasses lining the walls. This was a well-known establishment for the locals. Everyone in Tokushima who played a string instrument would come to this exact spot at one point or another. We stepped into the room in the back, which was set up like a consultation room, with four violins arranged in a neat row.

An "old violin" does not mean that it's merely old. It means that for however long it existed, it had been passed down from one musician to another and over the years, and matured to produce an exquisite sound. The wood ages with time and makes the sound deeper. And of course, since old violins are much rarer than new ones, they cost a whole lot more.

"Wow!"

"Asuka! Don't touch it!" My mother shot me a harsh look when I barely lifted a finger. Geez. Leave it to Mom to always say no. I turned to Mr. Kiyohara and said with my politest voice, "May I?"

"Sure, Asuka. Feel free to try whichever one you'd like."

"Great! What shall I play? How about *Twinkle, Twinkle, Little Star*?" I took the one that was closest to me and checked the tuning.

"Isn't *Twinkle, Twinkle, Little Star* a bit childish? Why don't you play one of the pieces that you're now practicing?"

"Okay. How about *Chaconne* ?"

After playing the piece for a while, I moved on to the next one.

"What do you think?" Mr. Kiyohara asked after I was done with the third one and was about to reach for the last.

"Well, the first one has a mellow sound that I do like, but the D string seems a little stiff and hard to get a proper sound. The second one is easy to play, but it has some unrefined timbre I don't care for. The third one isn't very good at all. It's hard to play, and it sounds stiff, too."

"Oh? I thought the third one was good. Don't you think these gold fixtures are beautiful?"

Of course, my mother would like the one that I didn't much care for.

"Mom, a violin isn't just about looks. You can always switch the fixtures, but you can't change the sound quality."

The appearance was important to my mother, and her typical remark irritated me. Effectively communicating to her my opinion, from my experience and perceptions, was something of a mission at the moment because I rarely got a chance to compare the sounds of old violins like these.

"Wel"You're not stilll, Asuka, you seem to have developed good ears. Go ahead, play the last violin now." "Wow, it looks ancient!"

Unlike the previous three, this last one was mottled all over and appeared to have some minor scratches to the tuning pegs. But on a closer look, I realized that it wasn't damaged. Someone had engraved the initials "DBL". I turned it over to check the back. The color of the wood had faded from the convex central part to where it would rest on your shoulder like it had been rubbed off. When I looked even closer, it appeared streaked with water stains. I wondered if the original owner had often cried while he or she played it.

"The fading on this one certainly shows its age."

"It was deliberately made to look old, like a seventeenth-century instrument, but actually, I was told that this was made in Germany in the early twentieth century, so it isn't that old. See those dots that look like blemishes? And the uneven color? They are additional touches to make it look antique. It certainly contributes to its value."

"I never would have imagined anyone would do that."

My mother looked intrigued, too.

With some trepidation and as if I were holding something mysterious, I played the A and E strings together.

"Whoa!"

For a moment, I thought my ears had deceived me. Layered on top of the soft timbre was another faint sound. Though the timbre was pleasant at first, it resonated with a particularly sad tone. This double resonance is usually caused by either a warped sound post, a flaw in the varnish, or a crack in the soundboard. But judging by the quality of the sound it produced, this violin couldn't have been defective.

"What is it?" my mother asked when I started peeking into the F-holes.

"It sounds a bit strange . . ."

"Sounded wonderful to me. Play some more for us, Asuka."

I began to play *Chaconne* as I did with the other three. No sooner had I played a single phrase than I realized it was completely different from any violin that I had ever touched.

"This violin is amazing! It sounds fantastic!"

"Yes, it is very good," Mr. Kiyohara said. "The wood has hardly dried properly to make it easy to play, but compared to the other century-old violins in Japan, I can tell that this had been stored in a dryer environment. That's why the sounds it produces are pretty extraordinary."

"I figured that violins like this existed. But there's something more . . ."

"Is it easy to bring out the desired sound, with that lovely resonance?"

"Exactly!"

Playing such a distinctive violin even a single time made all the others seem inferior. I finally understood what it meant when people said that finding a violin was a matter of fate.

"Mom, this is the one I want."

"That's easy for you to say. I can see that it's good, but doesn't it mean it's quite expensive?"

"Yes, ma'am, I paid a lot of money for it. I have no intention of selling it. However . . ." Mr. Kiyohara looked pensive for a moment and then said, "I could lend it to you. It is practically priceless, at least to me."

"Oh, no, such a valuable instrument is too good to my daughter."

My mother began to fret, but I already had my heart set on this intriguing violin. I was not ready to give it up.

"Now that I've played this, I can't think of any other."

"Be that as it may, only a professional would use such a precious violin."

"Perhaps that's true, Mrs. Murakami, but I can't guarantee that your daughter will ever find a violin better than this one. Finding the right instrument is all about a chance, and a personal connection. Even if you were to look at all the violins in a store before a competition, you may not find one that suits her desire,"

Mr. Kiyohara's words made me want the violin even more. His remark about chance and connection further strengthened my determination to have it.

"I still think it's too much for her to handle. I haven't seen her practice all that much lately."

"Mom, I promise I will practice a lot more. I'll start today, Mom. Please, please, please?"

"I still think it's too precious, just to have a child play for free."

Mr. Kiyohara stepped in. "How about this. Would you be willing to purchase insurance for it? I would be grateful if you can do that. Asuka, perhaps you will be able to buy this from me when you are older. What do you think?"

"I definitely will!"

While Mr. Kiyohara smiled, Mom looked flustered.

"To be perfectly frank, Asuka, there might be someone else who deserves this violin more than you do. But since you seem to have your heart set on it, I'm thinking that you are feeling a connection with it. It's an excellent violin. Play it well. You'll be able to produce better sounds that way. Promise me that you'll take exceptionally good care of it."

In the end, an arrangement was made for my mother to buy the insurance on the violin.

Perhaps it was because of my guilty conscience about using such a priceless violin like that, I practiced harder ever, though naturally, my desire to play as I pleased remained strong.

3

"Asuka, wouldn't you like to go back to Tokyo?"

My mother started pressing me about that again in early December, about six months after we got the violin. Sipping my cup of café au lait at the breakfast table, I glanced at her suspiciously. Any conversation that she struck up just before I left for school was usually unpleasant.

"Tokyo?"

I was well aware that she wasn't talking about going sightseeing or visiting theaters.

"You must surely realize that that's where the best universities are. If you're going to go into medicine, it wouldn't hurt to start thinking about the universities now."

"Mom, I've never said anything about wanting to become a doctor."

It was a tough topic for me to discuss with her, and I immediately lost my appetite. I put my half-eaten toast back on the plate and sighed.

"You're not still thinking about becoming a violinist? Seriously? Musicians in Japan hardly make ends meet. Many of them earn little to nothing. Here you are, thinking how great it would be if you could use your music skills to earn a living, but it is nearly impossible to survive in the competitive world of professionals."

"Okay, Mom."

I couldn't think of the right thing to say to her and became defensive. I had been practicing a lot more after getting the new violin, but I wasn't sure if I could say that I was putting my all into it and was aware that there would be a lot more ups and downs in the time to come.

The more I thought about a future as a professional violinist, the more

I felt pressured by the fear that I might not have the talent to do so. I was determined to do something in my life that involved the violin but refrained from setting any definite goals.

Sure, my mother said the road to becoming a professional soloist wouldn't be easy. I was well aware of that.

"You don't know if I could ever become a doctor either," I jumped to my feet and blurted.

"Aren't you going to finish your breakfast?"

"No."

I retreated to my room, grabbed my bag, and left. I heard my mother calling out to me but ignored her and headed for school.

For several days after that argument, I couldn't stop thinking that I might not have a natural aptitude for the violin. The practice had certainly been progressing more smoothly since getting my new violin six months earlier, and I had since been given two new pieces to practice.

They were Kreisler's *Variations on a Theme of Corelli in the Style of Tartini* and Schubert's *Ave Maria*. They looked simple enough at first, and though I had heard them being played many times and thought I could play them right away, the Corelli variations gave me a great deal of trouble.

No matter how hard I practiced, I simply couldn't come to terms with the series of three-part harmonies played simultaneously, or the quick tempo *Allegro*, so full of trills and similar ornaments. Though I wanted to put as much effort into *Ave Maria*, which I'd been assigned at the same time, it proved completely beyond me. I was struggling to make any progress on the latter. When I got to the octave harmonies that come in midway through *Ave Maria*, the fingers on my left hand refused to reach as far as I wanted them to. Even if I played slowly and paid close attention to the intervals, the shrill sounds I managed to produce were less akin to the violin than to the bagpipes or the Japanese panpipe called *sho*, thus making me less inclined to practice very long.

I finally concluded that I simply couldn't play *Ave Maria*. I went to many lessons without much practice. With no improvements in my skills, my normally patient teacher just pressed her hands against her ears and shouted, "Stop!"

With her shoulders slumped, she looked resigned as she continued,

"How about playing the octave harmony just once, and then trying to find the highest note?"

"Yes, ma'am, I'll do that."

It still didn't work. I couldn't produce a clear tone at all, and it discouraged me even more. This situation couldn't go on. I sometimes thought I could concentrate on *Ave Maria* if I mastered the Corelli variations, and other times I felt that I should just let go of *Ave Maria*.

I would have felt compelled to learn to play *Ave Maria* if it had been in my repertory book, but it wasn't. I didn't dislike it. It was just that I'd given up on it somewhere inside me as a work that I would never master. Because I had started out extra-motivated, I was both frustrated and frightened by this failure.

Mom seemed to think that long hours of practice would bring my skills up to the professional level, but that alone would not give me a deeper understanding of the pieces and wouldn't necessarily result in progress. I wondered how disappointed she'd be when she realized that I was just a mediocre player instead of the prodigy that I had once been regarded. Her expectations were exceedingly high, and I was afraid I wasn't good enough.

"Asuka, wait up!"

I heard the familiar voice behind me. I turned around and saw Ayumi, running with her school skirt shortened, even now in the middle of winter.

"Morning, Asuka. You're early today."

I waited for her to catch up, and we continued walking side by side.

"Yeah, Mom was being a pain in the neck, so I left early."

"You guys were fighting again?"

"She's always nagging me. She doesn't care how I feel."

I gave Ayumi a rundown on what had happened that morning as she listened and nodded. My irritation was somewhat soothed by having her listen quietly.

"You haven't been running over to my house lately," she said when I finished. "I know what you're going to say. I don't have that kind of time. I have to practice. Right, Asuka?"

"I have to make up for the time I've wasted blowing off steam. But still, it just isn't enough, no matter how hard I try."

"Oh," she said. "Does that mean you're serious? Aren't you going to be a doctor like your dad?"

"Well, the reason why I even considered it was because my dad uses big words like 'adrenaline' and 'dopamine,' which I always thought was cool. Once I understood words like that, it would be neat to sit and chat with him. But I don't like studying that much. I'd much rather spend ten hours a day on my violin."

"Then you're going to become a violinist?"

"I wonder how tough it is to become a soloist."

I was passionate about that. But effort alone will not be enough. How then could I do it? It was a tough question for a fourteen-year-old child like me.

4

I came home from school and received a visit from Mr. Kiyohara. He had come by to check the violin as part of the maintenance service they offered twice a year: once during the rainy season in early summer and again in December. Normally he would send one of his employees to do this but explained that he had come in person since he obviously had a special interest.

"Your practice isn't going very well?" he said as he scrutinized the instrument. "How can you tell?"

"Here, look at all these tiny granules of rosin that have worked their way into the upper end of the fingerboard. I would imagine that your bow is going askew when you play a harmony."

"That's exactly what my teacher says. When I get to the series of a three-part harmony in Corelli variations, my bow starts to do that and she tells me to raise it to a shorter distance. But it only helps a little."

Mr. Kiyohara nodded.

"My teacher said that people called you a prodigy when you were around my age. Why didn't you become a professional musician?"

"Why indeed. There was more than one reason for that, among which the biggest had been financial concerns. You see, Asuka, when I was around your age, I knew I had what it took to be up there, but it wasn't feasible. My parents operated a small shop that sold musical instruments, and they wouldn't have been able to pay for all the necessary expenses."

"Your parents . . ."

"But in your case, your family can afford it, and your mother seems supportive enough. If you're determined to pursue it as your career, your circumstances certainly are a great advantage."

I had never considered that. My mother may have always nagged me to practice, but after all, she was paying for my lessons. It dawned on me then that some children may want to play the violin but can't afford lessons, let alone the instruments.

"But Mr. Kiyohara, you still need talent. I'm practicing two pieces now, and the Corelli variations are giving me a lot of trouble. The other piece, *Ave Maria*, I'm making no progress at all . . ."

"What? You're practicing *Ave Maria*?"

"Yes. Why?"

Mr. Kiyohara seemed astonished. So much so that I stopped speaking and just looked at him.

"*Ave Maria* . . ." he repeated quietly before continuing. "The original owner of this violin was a girl your age. Her name was Hannah Janssen. She worked very hard on Schubert's *Ave Maria*, and this violin was given the nickname 'The Ave Maria Violin.'"

"A girl my age?"

"I don't know much about the details, but Hannah had been a survivor of Auschwitz, and I was told that this violin had been found in a poppy field right by the concentration camp."

"Auschwitz?"

"Oh, Asuka, don't you know about Auschwitz? Haven't you read *The Diary of Anne Frank*?"

"*The Diary of Anne Frank*..."

I had read a children's edition of the book when I was in elementary school, but all I knew was that Anne Frank was a girl who hid from the Nazis with her family in a secret room. I recalled that they were discovered by the Nazis in the end and sent to a concentration camp because her family was Jewish, but I never thought until this moment about what the Jewish people had done to deserve such treatment.

I was embarrassed that I knew nothing about history, particularly in foreign countries.   "I wonder if Hannah just abandoned her violin there. Why would she leave it?"

"Are you interested in her story, Asuka?"

"Of course, I am. She was the original owner of this violin, right? Why wouldn't I want to know about a girl my age who liked *Ave Maria*?"

"Well, then . . ."

The mere fact that a previous owner of this violin had been a girl my age felt like fate.

"The violin had been displayed in a private museum near Auschwitz before I bought it," Mr. Kiyohara said. "It was called 'The Ave Maria Violin.' I wanted to find out how it ended up in the museum, but the previous curator died before he told the whole story."

"So, you don't know?"

"Not yet, no. But I'm very interested in its history and have done some research. As it turns out, I might be able to meet a cellist who performed with Hannah."

"Really? Wow, that's amazing."

Mr. Kiyohara had checked sources like the German Tourism Association on the Internet, and eventually called a Polish radio station, which decided to do a phone interview with him on the air. He explained about the violin, that it had been left in the poppy field outside Auschwitz, and mentioned the name Hannah Janssen. A while later, he was contacted by a gentleman by the name of Calsas.

"In fact, he's coming to Japan to conduct Beethoven's 9th Symphony, and said he will gladly make time in his schedule to speak with me."

"Wow, Mr. Kiyohara, that sounds fantastic!"

"I would like you to come along too if your mother will allow you. I'm sure that Mr. Calsas would be pleased to meet you."

"Yes, I would love to."

I went straight to my mother, who was in the kitchen preparing dinner, and told her everything that Mr. Kiyohara had said. Mom was happy to allow me to meet this Mr. Calsas, readily accepting that hearing an Auschwitz survivor's account about escaping an unbelievable fate was much more valuable than my school studies. Perhaps she, too, was fascinated with the story of Hannah, the original owner of my violin. I didn't know at the time that my simple curiosity would change the direction that I would take in my life.

5

It was a snowy winter day a week later that I met Mr. Calsas.

Every year in December, Beethoven's 9th Symphony is performed by famous orchestras and small local ensembles throughout Japan. Our people love this piece and affectionately call it '*The Ninth*'. Mr. Calsas was coming to Japan to conduct one of those orchestras, and arrangements were made for us to go to Osaka to meet him.

Snow fell heavily outside when Mr. Kiyohara, my mother, and I visited the concert hall in Osaka during the rehearsal. People were bustling around the venue in preparation for the concert the following day. Mom and I must have stood out since people seemed to glance at us as they rushed past us. One man came rushing over after noticing us. He first approached Mr. Kiyohara, and after exchanging a few quick words, they walked over to the back room and invited me and Mom to join. It was a fairly large room, about 180 sq. ft. We felt a bit tense and entered quietly. In the back of the room sat an elderly gentleman with gray hair, who turned to look toward us.

Mr. Calsas was wearing an excellent quality beige suit with a burgundy scarf tied around his neck like a tie. I had previously been told that he was almost ninety years old, but he looked strong and healthy

Perhaps he had been anticipating our arrival; he stood up and embraced us—first, Mr. Kiyohara, then Mom, and then me. His hands shook a little as he took my hand in his; the hard, gnarled hands of an old man, nothing like the ones of someone who was accustomed to handling a musical instrument, and I found it a little intimidating.

As these initial impressions flitted through my mind, he said to me, not in German nor Polish, but in English, "I am Paul Calsas."

Then he said something that I figured were words of welcome. Mr. Kiyohara, who spoke both English and German, made introductions in English.

"Delighted to meet you," Mr. Kiyohara then said to Mr. Calsas in Japanese and they both smiled broadly.

"Mr. Calsas, we brought the Ave Maria Violin."

I set down the violin case that had been slung over my shoulder and opened the brand new burgundy covering.

"Do you have any doubt that this is it?" Mr. Kiyohara asked as he passed the violin to the old man.

Mr. Calsas took the violin and carefully examined it. His eyes narrowed beneath his long, white eyebrows, and his cloudy pupils seemed to shimmer with recollections of the distant past. In that husky, tremulous voice that's typical of the elderly, Mr. Calsas spoke to the violin.   "Ah, Hannah, at long last, we meet again. I wondered what happened when you disappeared from the museum. Have you found a happy home now? With this young lady?"

I got the impression that Mr. Calsas was seeing through the violin a young girl much like me. He wasn't speaking to the violin. He was speaking to Hannah through the violin.

"I have absolutely no doubt that this is the Ave Maria Violin that Hannah had owned. I took it to the Auschwitz museum after she died because I wanted to make sure that no one would ever forget the history of the place. I heard that a rumor had spread at one point that it was thrown away into the field at Auschwitz. I'm not sure who started telling such a thing."

"That's the story they told when it came up for auction in London," Mr. Kiyohara said.   Mr. Calsas gave a large nod as if he understood everything.

"I'm not sure how it came up for auction, but regardless, it must have been the fate of this violin. I'm glad that it's now in the hands of a Japanese girl—I hear the Japanese know how to take good care of things. How old are you, Asuka?"

I knew enough English to understand that he was asking my age, so I answered, "Fourteen."

"Oh!" Mr. Calsas exclaimed as he raised his head in delight. "It's uncanny. The same age that Hannah had been when I met her. She also slung her violin over her shoulder as you do. You're so much like her. You remind me of her. God must have brought this violin to you. How splendid! Could you play something for me?"

"Well, I'll play a little bit of *Ave Maria* . . ."

Being put on the spot was not suddenly going to improve my skills. I might have been able to play it a little better if it were the only piece I'd been practicing, but my performance was about average as usual, making me regret my lack of skills.

Since I didn't want to disappoint Mr. Calsas by playing a piece that would make him want to mute his ears, I played only single notes when it came to the part with the harmonies. "That's it..." Mr. Calsas said as he closed his eyes. He very slowly opened them when I finished performing as if to savor the lingering timbre. I looked at him and noticed that his eyes were welled up.

"You played that very well, Asuka. Almost as well as Hannah. It's as if you're the reincarnation of her."

I knew as well as anyone else that Mr. Calsas was being too generous with his praise. I appreciated his kindness. I promised to myself that I would practice harder.

6

As I finished playing, a member of the staff brought coffee for the adults and hot cocoa for me. Mr. Calsas sat back into his chair and sipped his coffee slowly, savoring it.

"Well, then, where shall I start with my story?"

Although the heat was turned up in the room, the air felt chilly with anticipation as Mr. Kiyohara, Mom, and I sat breathlessly, waiting to hear this elderly man tell us his tale. For a moment, the only sound we could hear was the muffled thud of the clumps of snow falling from the eaves right outside the window, which somehow made it disconcerting.

Mr. Calsas quietly began to speak between sips of coffee as steam rose from his cup.

"It's hard to believe the lifestyles that we now enjoy; drinking hot coffee on a cold winter's day like this is just a matter of course. You'd never imagine this is anything extraordinary, right, Mr. Kiyohara?"

Mr. Kiyohara sat completely still without so much as a nod.

"Asuka, the story I am about to tell might shock you, and you may find it hard to imagine." Mr. Calsas turned toward me again, but instead of the affectionate gaze he gave me a few moments earlier, he glanced at me with a hardened look.

"You have been living in comfort all your life. You wouldn't see how well off you really are. I hope that hearing my story today will help you live the rest of your life with more joy and gratitude. At the very least, I hope that you will understand what real happiness is. Do you study history in school?"

Luckily for me, Mr. Calsas chose his words carefully and spoke slowly, so I was able to follow most of what he was saying. But since my English wasn't good enough for me to know how to respond, I ended up simply saying, "Yes."

The old man fixed his gaze on the snow that was falling outside the window.

"All children need to study history. But simply learning things is worthless. You can memorize all sorts of timelines and charts about what happened during which year, but that doesn't mean that you KNOW anything about history. True studying is to take historical facts and to digest them in your own mind, to gain a true sense of what happened. Then you think about how we as human beings should live in the time to come, and consider the true meaning of happiness while keeping your eyes open to what's happening in the world and arrive at your own conclusions. That's what it means to truly study history."

Mr. Calsas set his coffee on the table and turned toward me.

"You now have possession of the 'Ave Maria Violin,' and you sling it over your shoulder like Hannah used to do." He narrowed his eyes and looked at me as if to take in my entire being with his gaze, and then drew a deep breath.

"You have lovely black hair. Hannah had blond hair. Her eyes were a deep, clear blue. The color of her eyes and the 'Ave Maria Violin' saved her from hell. Her older sister, younger brother, mother and father, and her grandmother and grandfather were all killed. As someone who has never seen hell or death, you probably wonder what all that has to do with you. So, what's tough for me is how I should go about properly conveying to you what it was like back then." Mr. Calsas sighed deeply, shrugged, and slowly shook his head from side to side.

"Asuka, how old is your grandfather?"

"Seventy."

As I wasn't sure about my English pronunciation, I held up seven fingers. Mr. Calsas nodded.

"Well then, this is a story from right around the time your grandfather would have been born. It begins in 1933. I wonder if you can imagine the time when your grandfather was just a baby, nursing from his mother's breast."

"Oh gross! I don't want to." I chuckled without thinking, and my mother and Mr. Kiyohara, who was interpreting, laughed, too.

Mr. Calsas smiled. "Indeed. That might not be something you would want to picture, but the important point is that you will have to imagine some very unpleasant things. It may be harder than memorizing historical facts for schoolwork, but I hope that it's for your own benefit. What I'm about to tell you will build character."

"Why do I have to build character?"

"That's a very good question, Asuka. You're living a good life, are you not? Every human being has the right to live happily. You do, your mother does, Mr. Kiyohara does, and so do I. However, though we all have the right to happiness, some are forced to the opposite. Let me ask you, Asuka, who do you think is happier, a person who is grateful when he or she drinks a good cup of coffee or a person who takes that cup for granted?"

"The grateful one."

"Exactly." Mr. Calsas looked pleased. "A person who takes things for granted may be living a wealthy lifestyle. On the contrary, a person could find happiness in a good cup of coffee, even if they barely have any possessions. Building character means nurturing your soul to feel all emotions, including happiness. It's about empathy and being a person who can convey that feeling to others. You can't do this by simply daydreaming. Every one of us has a duty to experience a variety of things, and to exercise our minds and our soul."

Neither Mr. Kiyohara, Mom, nor I spoke. We were mesmerized by what the elderly man was saying.

7

"What happened to Hannah?"

"Ah, yes. It was on a cold winter day like today, in 1933 when the Nazi Party achieved a parliamentary majority. Adolph Hitler was appointed Chancellor of Germany, which turned out to be the gateway to hell."

"In Japan, when the representative of the majority party is chosen, he becomes the Prime Minister. That's what happened there?"

After I found out that I was going to meet Mr. Calsas, I reread *The Diary of Anne Frank*. This time, it wasn't the children's edition, but the full version. It's rather difficult to get a good understanding of history set in foreign countries because, for one thing, you don't live there. Just as Mr. Calsas said, I would understand things better if I could get someone else's perspectives.

"Yes, that's exactly right, Asuka. Politics is a fearsome thing. Don't ever be indifferent about who runs your country." Mr. Calsas shifted his gaze for a moment as if to recall a distant memory and began to talk about the time he met Hannah.

"The Nazis began persecuting the Jews soon after Hitler assumed his position. It was a terrible time not only for the Jews but also for many others including the Poles and the Russians. By the time Hannah was old enough to go outside on her own to play, she was no longer allowed to do so, and there was hardly ever enough food on the table."

"Was she poor?"

"No. Hannah's family owned a grocery shop and were far from poor. Her parents were hard-working people and built a successful business. Her mother used to be a schoolteacher but had to stop teaching to help with the shop when Hannah's grandmother became ill and was confined to a wheelchair. As she could play the piano, she gave lessons every Sunday to the children in the neighborhood. Hannah also had a brother about nine years younger, though I don't think the poor boy ever saw much daylight."

Mr. Calsas continued to tell Asuka how Hannah had learned to play the violin at a very young age. She used to prance along the street playing polkas and waltzes, twirling around merrily. Asuka imagined the neighbors being entertained by the little girl.

Chapter 2: The Janssen Family

1

The neighbors often called out to Hannah when she walked down the street: "Hi, Hannah. What songs did you learn today?" "It's Grandpa's birthday today. Come over and play a piece for him tonight."

Although Hannah was still a young child, she acted as if she were already an accomplished violinist, and performed for anyone who asked. This helped to enhance her repertoire, and it didn't take her very long to earn a reputation as a prodigy.

Hannah's older sister Nina was often sick and had a bad leg. Hannah loved Nina dearly and looked after her well, often holding her hand to help her get around. The love was mutual. Nina knitted gloves and a scarf for Hannah when it got cold. Hannah was always bright and cheerful, and she was loved by everyone in the neighborhood. Nina was proud of the social butterfly that her younger sister proved to be.

The days went by unchanged, giving no reason to believe that the sun wouldn't shine as it always did—until that particular day in 1933.

That was when the doors to hell opened. Jewish people were forbidden from stepping out of their homes in the evening. Then came an order that prohibited them from owning radios. The secret Nazi police, known as the Gestapo, could suddenly barge in during dinner to destroy people's radios and verify the identities of Jewish residents. Should any family member be absent, the Gestapo would step into the bathroom or shower or wherever and drag them out, even if they were in the middle of taking care of business. They were forced to stand at attention without making the slightest move until the identities of everyone in the household had been verified. Many professionals like doctors and lawyers, no longer able to work, were quick to flee abroad.

Next, the Jews were forced to wear a yellow Star of David on their chests so they could be identified. This made them subject to abuse from German civilians, among whom the heartless ones would throw stones or spit at them. Then, they imposed a curfew on the Jews, so it became harder for them to go out freely. Under such oppression, Hannah's family managed to continue to operate their shop and led their lives in a relatively normal way. Hannah was ten years old at the time. Then one day in 1938, the Gestapo came to the synagogues and smashed the stained-glass windows, and destroyed stores that were operated by Jews, including the Janssens' shop. This was known as Kristallnacht because all the shards of broken glass strewn about the streets sparkled like bits and pieces of crystal.

Hannah's father shouted at her mother to flee, but the moment she and Nina, with her disability, filled their arms with what little they could carry from the shop, they were seized by the Gestapo. One of the merciless officers pointed a pistol at Nina's head.

Shocked, Mrs. Janssen clung to Nina and pleaded with him to spare her daughter. An officer kicked Mrs. Janssen with his riding boots, making her tumble backward. The riding boots must have been ridden with spurs, as her clothes were torn and soaked in blood.

Nina was ordered to stand and walk out of the shop but was so terrified that she could barely move her feeble legs. She somehow managed, dragging her bad leg behind. The officers watched and laughed.

"What a worthless creature!" one of them exclaimed, and unleashed two enormous dogs. Nina had no chance of escape. The dogs attacked her, sinking their teeth into the thigh of her bad leg. Her agonized screams echoed throughout the surrounding streets.

Powerless to protect his daughter, Mr. Janssen sank beneath the counter, covered his ears, and prayed. He felt like a coward, but there was nothing he could do. Mrs. Janssen couldn't join him, as she had fainted. Nina, though barely breathing, was still alive.

"Oh, you poor thing," a Gestapo said to her. "I'll give you a treatment that will end your suffering." He drew his pistol and shot her in the chest. The sound echoed throughout the neighborhood as the sun slowly set, causing the bystanders to be at a loss for words. The single shot that had just killed a young girl sent shivers through the heart of everyone that witnessed this terrible deed.

They trembled with fear as the blood flowed from Nina's body to soak the ground bright crimson. The glow of the setting sun on the blood-stained street heightened the sense that what had once been a peaceful neighborhood instantly become a scene of terror. Nina became the first victim in their small town.

Once the Gestapo left, her mother and father, wailing with anguish over their inability to save their daughter, took her lifeless body in their arms. They were too late. Nina no longer opened her eyes.

From that day onward, the Gestapo wreaked their havoc upon them day in and day out until the bodies of their victims became a common sight in the neighborhood. There were many cases of entire families being killed because one of them had not been present during an inspection. Bodies were tossed onto the streets, where they were soon covered with maggots and rats that feasted on their flesh, giving off an acrid stench. In just over a week, the town became a place where it was no longer possible to live a normal life. It was around this time that the surviving Jews and Poles were rounded up and sent to concentration camps.

On one evening, ten days after losing their oldest daughter, the Janssens decided to quietly leave and take refuge in a neighboring town. Taking only what they could carry, they snuck out of their house two at a time so as not to attract attention. Mr. Janssen and his elderly mother were the last to leave. He began to quietly push the wheelchair. Just then, in the distance, there were loud stomping of Gestapo's jackboots. Someone must have turned them in.

The elderly Mrs. Janssen realized that she could no longer escape.

"My son, I am a burden on you. The family needs you to look after them, and they shouldn't lose you because of me. I am ready to meet my end. Take the back door. Quickly!"

Having helplessly watched his daughter being murdered, the thought of leaving his mother to die was more than Mr. Janssen could bear. But there was no time to lose if he wanted to see to the safety of the rest of his family. He kissed his mother one last time, took the Bible from his bag, and pressed it into his mother's wrinkled hands.

"What are you doing? Son, this is no time to drag your feet!" She scolded him in a low voice so no one else would hear her. Mr. Janssen was aware that he now had to leave or else he, too, would be captured by the Gestapo and endanger the lives of the rest of his family.

Mr. Janssen turned and fled. The matriarch of the family closed her eyes and quietly began to say her final prayers as two Gestapo officers smashed the store entrance and started making their way upstairs.

"Where is your family?"

Her eyes were closed as she made not the slightest movement. She continued to whisper her prayers, which gave her the strength to maintain her composure.

"Is she deaf? Senile" One of the officers blurted, thrusting his jaw out at the old woman as the Bible trembled in her hands.

"You've been abandoned, you poor old hag!" Another officer slowly began pushing her wheelchair to the edge of the staircase. He stopped for a moment, then kicked it with his jackboot. The wheelchair gained momentum as she tumbled down the stairs. The devout Jewish woman fell to her death without uttering so much as a whimper, perhaps determined to ensure that her fleeing son would not hear her and stop in his tracks. The heavy wheelchair was soon lying crushed at the bottom of the stairs, where the old woman lay crumpled, yet dignified to the end. The Gestapo officers roared with laughter.

2

His coffee had gotten cold as Mr. Calsas told his story. He sipped it and shrugged.

Asuka had seen some documentaries and movies on television about the persecution of the Jews, but hearing the account from someone who had lived through it was much more powerful.

"They toyed with human lives as if they were nothing more significant than worms," Mr. Kiyohara said, voicing the mutual sentiment of the Japanese visitors.

"Less than worms."

"Mr. Calsas, why were the Germans so cruel?"

"It's not that all Germans were bad, because individually, they were wonderful people. Asuka. The important thing to understand is that when people are organized into large groups, sometimes even an average person can be capable of cruelty. I think it's human nature. We can never be like God. But you and I can be different. We will never succumb to such impulses."

"But how can you be so sure? We will never know how God would act."

"Because we have the power of music. Close your eyes for a moment and play Chopin's *Tristesse* in your head."

Despite her very limited English ability, Asuka managed to understand what he was saying. She closed her eyes. She somehow felt as if she was lulled in a cozy, warm world. She had experienced a similar sense of security before, she thought—perhaps a distant memory as an infant cuddled in her mother's arms. Her eyes remained closed as she listened to Mr. Kiyohara interpreting what Mr. Calsas was saying.

"This is the reason why we practice our music. If you skip practices and try to fake your way through, the music will never resonate with your heart. But if you play every day, there will be a time when you would feel the love of God.

When that happens, there is no way you would ever betray God's love."

Mr. Kiyohara nodded in agreement.

Asuka was touched. She was grateful to learn what it meant to be engaged in music. Hearing this from a survivor of Auschwitz made her understanding of the true meaning of music all the more significant.

"The Germans love music so much that they would be lost without it. That's the reason why Hannah was able to come out of Auschwitz alive."

"But if their love of music was so great, they wouldn't end up being such horrible people, would they?"

"Asuka, loving music and having music in your heart are entirely different things. Many people love music, and they try to control it. But we're aware that music has a life of its own. If you play music when you're upset, it will sound angry, and if you play music when you're feeling love, it will sound loving. They say that the eyes are the window of the soul. So is music. Whether you are feeling pride, suspicion, jealousy, or some other emotion, it will come out in the tonal quality of your music. We're given the opportunity to reflect on these things through music. That's the big difference between people who only listen to music and those who play it. Do you understand what I'm saying?"

Asuka could relate. She smiled and nodded. Mr. Calsas smiled back.

"I've gotten old and returned to Poland, but had lived in the United States before that. There was once a big article in the New York Times that mentioned a Japanese music teacher among five celebrities that were visiting. It caught my interest. I heard that there was a concert at Carnegie Hall where this teacher's students would be performing, so I went to watch."

Mr. Calsas said the children ranged from age five to around Asuka's age, though they may have been a bit older. Asians tend to look younger. He said they had impeccable manners and made him wonder what such youngsters would perform. He was stunned when they played concertos and sonatas as skillfully as adult professionals.

Overwhelmed by the beauty of their music, tears rolled down his cheeks.

He felt the presence of God through those children.

"I knew from the high standards of their performance that they must have been raised in happy homes. If not for music, they might have grown up to be arrogant, but I was given the impression that through music, they were already growing up with very cultured minds. They were like little angels to me. The instructor who was accompanying the children appeared to be fairly old but walked with firm steps. I learned that his wife was German. I was amazed by their performance. I can still recall it like it happened yesterday."

That was ten years after he had been freed from the concentration camp. He had relocated to the United States to leave his past. He wanted to forget about the horrible war. His life had finally started to become somewhat more peaceful. He was beginning to feel at ease. After constantly being plagued by the hell that he had been through, the concert at Carnegie Hall made him feel as if he was reborn.

"I wondered if Japan was a country that was given a mission by God to advocate for peace. That's why I was thrilled to learn that I would be meeting with you on this visit. I think that if the United States is the father who can win peace and freedom through his determination, then Japan is the mother who can heal your wounds with her gentle embrace."

"You're not going to believe this, Mr. Calsas," Mr. Kiyohara said. "I was one of the children who performed at Carnegie Hall!"

"You were?" Mr. Calsas rose from his seat and exclaimed in astonishment.

He then slowly began to pace around the room and continued with his story.

3

"Hannah's family spent nearly a year living in the basement of a house that belonged to a German family they knew in the next town over, in Berlin."

It was a two-story house painted white. From the foyer to the right, was the staircase to the second floor. The dining room was at the far-left corner of the house. Outside of the dining room window was a spacious lawn, edged with blueberry bushes.

The basement was directly beneath the dining room. A narrow staircase beneath the trap door was the only access. The homeowners stored wine and food supplies. The room was only about 200 square feet, with no windows nor adequate ventilation which made it somewhat musty. But with its entrance covered by a thick rug and the dining table placed on top, it had been the safest place to hide. Hannah, her mother and father, her brother Andrew, and her grandfather lived in that small room. Andrew was only three years old at the time.

Mr. Janssen had neither witnessed his mother's death nor gone back to check on her. He told the rest of his family that she was being cared for by a nice family nearby because she couldn't have gotten away. But he knew the obvious fate of his mother. The guilt from his failure to protect his mother, as well as his eldest daughter, laid heavily on him. He could not get the image of Nina's final moment out of his head. He started drinking more and more with agony.

As most of the residents in the town were Germans, the police roundups were not nearly as severe as what the Janssens had seen back in their old neighborhood. Still, the Gestapo conducted their inspections twice a month to ensure that no Jews were hiding among the townspeople.

Since everyone knew that the Gestapo would not be coming back for a while after an inspection, the Janssen children were allowed to venture up to the first floor to enjoy some sunlight through the windows but had to hurry back down if any visitor came by. The curtains that covered the windows facing the street made the room dim, and because permanently closed drapes would arouse suspicion, the homeowners would intentionally open the windows and sing German folk songs when they heard the sounds of Gestapo jackboots clicking on the streets. The sound of a window being opened and two thumps on the floor were the signals they used to warn the Janssens to hide without making a sound.

Hannah enjoyed this game of hide-and-seek. Andrew, on the other hand, was afraid to go upstairs without his mother. Even when his sister was upstairs, the little boy often chose to stay down. Mrs. Janssen was concerned that Andrew might develop rickets. But because she was far more concerned about losing her tiny angel, she couldn't force him to go upstairs.

Since the slightest flame was out of the question in the basement for risk of carbon monoxide poisoning, the family ate dinners that their German hosts cooked for them.

It meant that if guests stopped by the house in the afternoon, the Janssens would skip a meal, which happened from time to time, and because the children would become irritated with hunger, Mrs. Janssen ate only a third of her bread and saved the rest as emergency provisions. She would also open a bottle of wine, let it sit so the alcohol would evaporate, and dip stale bread in the wine so it would be more palatable for her children.

The woman who hid the Janssens was Mrs. Berger, Hannah's violin teacher. The house was just over a mile from Hannah's old neighborhood. Hannah used to walk to and from Mrs. Berger's house for her lessons. Being a young girl with a small frame, Hannah could only walk so fast, and it was rather a long trip for her back then, but after the lessons, she used to skip with joy all the way home. Hannah's skills quickly improved. She quickly learned one piece after the other.

Mrs. Berger was kind, and lighthearted in nature. She had met her husband while playing in an orchestra in Berlin that he conducted. She had since left the orchestra and was teaching the violin at home. Mr. Berger often traveled abroad for concerts. The couple had no children.

Hannah was one of Mrs. Berger's favorite students. She always came to her lessons well prepared. Mrs. Berger heard what happened to Hannah's poor sister. It was she who suggested that Hannah and her family hide at her home.

Mr. Janssen refused her offer at first, saying he could not involve the Bergers in their predicament. But as the situation grew worse and it became impossible to raise his children amid the terror and corpses strewn on the streets, he finally decided to accept the offer.

The Gestapo were constantly patrolling the streets interrogating Jews by the time the curfew was in place for the Jews. Some of the townspeople began to suggest that the Jews should simply be killed off. Even before they went in hiding, except for some minimal errands, the Janssens had simply stopped going out.

Hannah was unable to go to her lessons for several months but was able to play at home what she had learned, to her mother's piano accompaniment. Mrs. Berger would get in touch with Hannah's mother and tell her what Hannah should work on. Thus, Hannah practiced trills, vibrato, and harmonies, over and over again. She would modulate her playing without attempting to rush ahead, for she thought the day would soon come when she could resume her lessons with Mrs. Berger. Although Hannah started to get bored of playing the same things repeatedly, it was this practice that helped her hone her skills. This period may have been what nurtured her talent. After moving to the Bergers' basement, as soon as the Gestapo left the area, Hannah poured her soul into the violin. She felt fortunate to have Mrs. Berger as her private instructor for her daily practices.

Mrs. Berger always gave Hannah praises. She didn't scold her if the notes were off pitch. But she would tap Hannah's left fingers with the tip of a pencil if Hannah continued, pretending not to notice.

"Don't deceive yourself! Your conscience is the voice of God."

Hannah didn't know that it was a quote from Tolstoy, but it was etched in her mind.

Mrs. Berger assigned Hannah Wagner's Tannhäuser and other pieces that were popular with the military because they extolled Germany. Hannah also had to memorize these pieces so she could play them by heart wherever she was, which meant that her lessons had to be stricter. Her father was getting fed up with the selections and asked Mrs. Berger why his daughter had play pieces that lauded Germans over and over again.

"Mr. Janssen," Mrs. Berger said. "We will not cause them to be suspicious, as long as Hannah plays these pieces. We'll be okay, even with all those German soldiers patrolling outside. And if there is an unfortunate turn of events, the music will help her daughter to survive. Would you not agree?"

Mr. Janssen realized the depth of Mrs. Berger's affection for Hannah and felt indebted.

"Don't worry. The Germans become as docile as kittens when you play music for them. She'll be fine. As for Andrew, he's a little on the small side. We could get him to start practicing on a small violin in a little while. I'd like to have him play at least one piece."

"But Mrs. Berger, we have barely any money left to pay for Hannah's monthly lessons. You not only refuse to accept payments, but you have even provided us with food. We could never ask for more."

"Don't worry about it, Mr. Janssen, it's a minor issue. My husband is a highly sought-out orchestra conductor. We live comfortably. I only charge my other students because they wouldn't practice if I didn't. Now, Mr. Janssen, my husband will be coming home at the end of the month. Let's have Hannah give us an evening concert. I would like my husband to see how much she has improved. She really is a genius at the violin. She's skilled enough that if it weren't for the conditions today, she would have made her debut a long time ago. My husband will be amazed. Would you ask your wife to help me prepare some food and provide a piano accompaniment?"

Mr. Janssen held Mrs. Berger's hand in his to convey his heartfelt gratitude.

4

The day of Hannah's make-shift concert finally arrived. With the Gestapo leaving three days earlier, it had been quiet. Mrs. Berger heard awful rumors about Hannah's old neighborhood, but never mentioned them to the Janssens. They were probably aware of what was happening but did not dare to bring it up.

"I'm happiest when I'm cooking. Thank you so much for letting me help you," Mrs. Janssen said as she made thin apple slices and filled tart shells.

"It's a pleasant diversion. And you let my husband's father weed the garden, allow my husband to help with the cleaning so none of us would get bored—I don't know how to thank you for your thoughtfulness."

"Oh, don't mention it. I'm the one who's enjoying your company. I was often alone and feeling lonely."

Mr. Berger arrived home as the women talked. "I'm Home! Oh, our home smells wonderful."

Mrs. Janssen had heard so much about him and developed an image of the man in her mind, but was surprised as he was much more dashing than she had expected. Mr. Berger had deep blue eyes and chestnut-colored hair that was a little long. He wore a beard that joined at his sideburns, his mild features reminded her of Schumann. He had a vibrant smile. This was the man who was received well from the male-dominant society led by Hitler and his military.

"Welcome home, honey. You look like a hungry bear just out of hibernation." Mrs. Berger watched her husband inhale deep to smell the food in the kitchen and chuckled. Mr. Berger rushed over to embrace her. He noticed that her hands were covered with butter. Nonetheless, he gave her a deep kiss.

"It's a pleasure to meet you, Mr. Berger. We've been able to enjoy our time here because of your generosity. We cannot thank you enough."

"Pleasure to meet you too, Mrs. Janssen. I'm the grateful one, for you've been keeping my wife company."

Mr. Berger held Mrs. Janssen's hand, which was also covered with butter, and gave it a light kiss.

"Oh, my, excuse my greasy hand."

"Well, he has to wash up anyway. Right, honey? Why don't you do that so we can eat."

Mr. Berger made a show of sucking in his stomach, making the women break out into laughter.

The supper began at five o'clock. It was the first time for the Bergers and the Janssens to gather around the same table. Although it was a simple meal of oatmeal, cheese, beer, sausage, bread, and potatoes, the offer of hot food and second servings made the Janssens feel as if they were in heaven. Mr. Berger had learned of the Janssens' situation in his wife's letters, and had brought gifts of chocolate for Hannah and Andrew. Andrew was reluctant to venture upstairs because he always associated it with scary people, but the chocolate made him forget about his fears.

Mr. Berger's workload had increased since the war began. Though he no longer went on tours to enemy countries like the United States, he was taking more trips to German army camps, which had boosted his fame in the military by holding him in high regard.

"There was a concert at Nazi headquarters the day after Hitler merged Austria with Germany. The concertmaster—the violinist who sits on the left of the orchestra just in front of the first row of the audience—one of the strings on his violin snapped right at the opening phrase of Beethoven's Fifth Symphony, *da da da dah*. Someone immediately brought him a new violin, but another string snapped at the end of the fourth *da da da dah*, and they quickly brought him another violin. Hitler approached the concertmaster and whispered something in his ear. No more strings snapped after that. Or perhaps I should say that no one was worried about more strings snapping. Do you know why?"

"Because the violin was scared of Hitler?" asked Andrew, crossing his small hands in front of him and shuddered.

Mr. Berger saw how frightened Andrew had become, dabbed blueberry jam over a biscuit, and carried it to his little mouth.

"That's right. It's just as you say. I asked him afterward what Hitler had said, and he said Hitler told him that he'd be shipped off to a concentration camp if he broke another string. He pretended to play the violin so it would never break. The occurrence on that day made everyone very good at their vibratos," Mr. Berger said with a grin.

Had it been two years since they had last felt so carefree around the dinner table? The Janssens laughed like there was no tomorrow, knowing that they soon needed to go back to the dreary basement.

For little Andrew, who had always been told to keep his voice down, this was the first time for him to see his entire family laughing loud while they ate a meal. At first, Andrew blinked in astonishment, but soon enough he was holding his stomach and laughing out loud like everyone else. Although he probably had no idea why everyone was laughing, he joined the laughter at the top of his lungs which made Mrs. Berger laugh even harder.

It was around eight o'clock when the wives served apple tarts, tea, and an assortment of fruits. Andrew was so happy to see the array of desserts that he began to jump up and down on the sofa and received a scolding from his father.

"Hannah, why don't you go ahead and show us your talent now?" Mr. Berger suggested as he sat back on the sofa.

Hannah played Mozart's *Rondo*, Pugnani's *Largo Espressivo*, followed by Pachebel's *Canon* to Mrs. Berger's accompaniment. Mrs. Janssen, on the piano, was amazed at how her daughter had improved.

"The final piece I'm going to perform tonight is Schubert's *Ave Maria*."

Because of the persecution that she had experienced, Hannah was unlike Mrs. Berger's other students. A slower, more emotional piece seemed to better suit her. As she performed *Ave Maria*, the slow, clear tones seemed to elevate different emotions within each of them.

"Bravo, Hannah, that was excellent. Play it for us again," Mr. Janssen said, embracing Hannah as his eyes brimmed with tears.

Mr. Berger felt immensely satisfied. He couldn't help but feel vexed that Hannah's budding talent, which not only could have made her the star of any orchestra but a world-class soloist, had nowhere to go.

"Hannah, you are a marvelous violinist. But there's one thing that you still have to work on. In a piece like *Ave Maria*, you should put all your emotions into your moves as you use the bow as you move gradually from a low register to a high register," Mr. Berger said, instructing her to use the full bow from tip to heel. While a clever performer can produce adequate results through superficial movements, he didn't want Hannah to play like that. She paid close attention to what she was told and played the piece again from the nineteenth to the twenty-third bar.

"Yes, that's it. Concentrate on playing smoothly all the way. Don't let your vibrato waver. Now, try playing from the beginning again. Oh, and let's not forget to put your heart into it. Play this piece like all your desires depend on it."

Hannah closed her eyes. Her mother started to play a soft piano accompaniment. Hannah allowed her thoughts to drift back to a typical day in the past when she had been happy. Baking cookies with her mother and her sister. The morning her brother was born.

I do not need a special day. All I want is for everyone to have their normal days back.

She played the refrain for the third time while silently making her innocent wish with all her heart as she ended the piece in a long decrescendo.

Mr. Berger was speechless. He couldn't even manage to applaud.

"Mr. Berger?"

Mr. Berger slowly opened his eyes, got up from the sofa, and wrapped his arms gently around Hannah's small shoulders.

"Hannah, you are amazing. That was unreal. It made me feel like I was surrounded by a host of angels and lifted to heaven. I have nothing else to teach you. Always remember this: No matter where or in what situation you play, always put your heart and soul into the music. Music is a living thing that can move people's hearts. As I always tell my orchestra, the world of music has nothing to do with politics or war. It only exists in heaven, with God, and in our conscience. That's why people never cease to love music. Those who live a conscientious life are spiritually more fulfilled, and even bad people would wish to be saved—by the *Ave Maria* that you play."

Hannah was very happy to hear that. An even greater joy awaited her.

"By the way, Hannah, you are outgrowing your violin. Your fingers will get cramped if you don't start playing a full-size instrument," Mr. Berger reached beneath the sofa and pulled out a full-size violin case.

"Go ahead and open it. It's a gift for you."

Mrs. Janssen was astonished and politely refused, saying she and her family could not take further advantage of his generosity. Mr. Berger dismissed her concerns with a wave of his hand. He opened the case for Hannah, who was hesitant about accepting it.

"Wow! Is this an antique?" Hannah asked as she held the violin in her left hand and gazed at it.

"No, it's not. It's relatively new, but it was made by an expert craftsman to create an antique-style finish. It took him two years to make this, and it's made to look like the ones that were made in Cremona during the sixteenth century. But that's not all. With this rounded soundboard, it produces a sweet, mellow sound like an Amati, yet has deep resonance. That's why I liked it and bought it—though, of course, I hadn't told my wife about it."

Mrs. Berger laughed. "Oh, you!" She took the violin from Hannah and tuned it for her. "Oh? What's this? There's an engraving on the pegs. D. B. L."

"Ah, yes. Paul, the maker of this violin, engraved that. It stands for '*Das Beste Leben*'—'The Best Life'."

Mrs. Berger nodded in acknowledgment and plucked a string to check the tuning. "My goodness."

"You see?" Mr. Berger said smugly. "Hannah, would you play the opening bars of *Largo Espressivo* for me?" Mrs. Berger requested, handing the violin back. Hannah did as her teacher said and played the first seven bars. The sound was lovelier than she had imagined, and she instantly fell in love with her new violin.

"Why don't you play a little more, until I tell you to stop?"

Mrs. Berger enjoyed the music so much that she forgot to tell Hannah to stop. "Sorry, Hannah. I was absorbed in your performance."

"Thank you, Mr. Berger. I'll take good care of it." Holding the violin in her arm, Hannah bent her knees and curtsied.

Hannah's grandfather, who had been silently watching this exchange, spoke for the first time since arriving at the Berger residence.

"Mr. Berger, thank you very much for picking out a truly fine violin for my granddaughter. I don't know, though—we can't continue to take advantage of your generosity. This is too much. We wanted to give Hannah a violin ourselves. Would you at least accept payment for the violin?"

"With all due respect, I think you should hold onto as much money as you can. It's already starting to become impossible to use Jewish money," Mr. Berger said.

"As a proprietor of a store, we managed to exchange all our money into Reichsmark. We would really like to do this for Hannah. As something for her to remember us by," her father added.

"Oh, please, you shouldn't worry about anything like that. I'm sure we'll be able to go back to our normal lives after we wait out. God would not allow something like this to continue," Mrs. Berger said.

"The violin is expensive, the bow is expensive, and so is that leather case. Please, allow us to at least pay for the violin. We would not be able to stay here with you otherwise," Hannah's mother said.

"All right. Hannah, this violin is filled with the sentiments of everyone in your family. As long as you have it, you should always be able to remember your family when you grow up and leave home."

"Thank you so much, Mr. Berger. I wish my wife could have watched Hannah perform today," the elder Mr. Janssen remarked.

"It's getting late, Father. Let's clean up and head on back to the basement." Mr. Janssen said as if to cut off the old man's words.

"If there's anything you need while you're in the down there, please don't hesitate to come to us. And Andrew, I hope you'll get used to us, and come upstairs with your sister. I have a one-sixteenth-size children's violin that one of my students outgrew just the other day. Why don't you try your hand at it?" Mrs. Berger asked.

"Oh my, we truly appreciate that, Mrs. Berger. As for our time in the basement, we have peace of mind, and I can't think of anything more that we could ask for," Mrs. Janssen said.

Mrs. Berger opened a small violin case that had been set against one of the piano legs and placed it on Andrew's left shoulder. "Here, hold it steadily with your neck. That's it. Now stretch out your left arm. Can you hold the scroll at the end?"

Andrew clenched the violin between his chin and shoulder when it began to slip and carefully stretched out his left arm.

"It fits you perfectly. Let's start practice tomorrow. We'll begin by supporting the violin between your shoulder and your chin."

Delighted, Andrew began to skip around. Hannah's home concert appeared to have erased his fear of venturing upstairs.

"Thank you so much for everything. We could never repay you for your kindness. God bless you and your husband." Hannah's grandfather removed the kippah from his head and made a deep bow.

Andrew's lessons began the following day. For about ten days, he was able to go upstairs, feeling safe. Perhaps because he had been watching his sister practice, he did much better than she had. He was able to steady the violin after practicing for four days and began to make sounds, even when it was pulled away from him.

"The thinnest string is called the E string. Try playing it."

Andrew drew the bow across the string from top to bottom. A screech sounded.

"That's good, Andrew. But it's different from the sound your sister makes. Would you show him, Hannah? Without vibrato?"

Hannah had just started practicing on the full-size violin. It produced considerably louder sounds compared to her previous three-quarter-size instrument.

"Well, Andrew?"

"It's clear. Not screechy."

"Yes, good, you can tell the difference. Which do you think sounds better, the sound that you make or what your sister just produced?"

"My sister's, of course," he said, looking at his sister with admiration in his eyes. Although Hannah was his older sister, he had never admired her or paid any particular attention to her. She was a lot older. This was the first time he noticed how amazing his sister was.

"All right, let's try to make the sound as your sister does. Now, Andrew, you're touching the bow to the string too lightly, and that's why you can only make it screech. How can I explain it? Put the violin down for a moment." Mrs. Berger attached a tin toy car to the end of the bow with a rubber band.

"Yay."

"The end of the bow feels a little heavier now, doesn't it? Draw it straight between the fingerboard and the bridge. Don't bend your back. Spread your legs out, don't falter."

The sound that he made became more like a whistling tone.

"That's good. Don't forget that sound. You have talent. Now, let's have your sister play *Twinkle, Twinkle, Little Star*. I'd like you to play just the rhythm, going thump-thump, on the A and E strings."

Andrew did his best to keep up with Hannah's playing with the thump-thump-thumps. "I did it." He held his violin in his left hand and jumped around in excitement.

Andrew learned to play *Twinkle, Twinkle, Little Star* within a month. He discovered the joy of playing the violin and missed it when the risky days drew near. For Andrew, the small violin was his sole toy and friend. Although he pleaded with his parents about bringing it down to the basement, it was not to be, as any sounds overheard by others could put not only the Janssens but also the Bergers in danger.

Andrew received chocolates and fruits as a treat when he went upstairs, and he could hardly wait to resume his lessons. The Gestapo frequented the area, and he was happy when he could resume his lessons when they left. But on those days that Gestapo were at their door, he wasn't allowed to go upstairs, for the fear that they could come back.

Having listened to his sister playing violin all his life, Andrew had grown up with an innate ear for music. Proof of this was his ability to play a piece from memory after playing it a few times. Mrs. Berger was delighted that Andrew turned out to be another outstanding student of hers and looked very much forward to the progress of the Janssen children.

Andrew was able to play Gossec's *Gavotte* three months later. Mr. Berger, a former cellist, provided accompaniment while Mrs. Berger and Hannah played the second violin, allowing Andrew to become a fully adequate new member of their home orchestra.

Mr. Berger's month-long leave eventually came to an end, and he went back on another concert tour.

6

One evening two days after Mr. Berger had left, a cat could be heard outside the front door. Mrs. Berger opened the door and found a skinny Siamese sitting on the doorstep. On closer look, the cat's whiskers were very short, as if someone had cut them off. She felt very sorry for the cat.

"Where did you come from? You must be hungry."

Mrs. Berger picked up the cat and brought it inside the house. She poured a small amount of milk into a saucer, and the cat drank it all, its eyes closed in bliss, and continued to lick the saucer after the milk was gone, so she poured more into the saucer. The cat drank it in an instant and would not stop crying, so she went into the kitchen and tore off some dried meat, which the cat quickly downed.

It must have been starving. Apparently satisfied, it began to lick its paws and wash itself. Mrs. Berger took the cat back outside, but as it showed no sign of leaving, she brought it back inside, thinking that it would be a good friend for Hannah and Andrew.

Hannah and Andrew always came upstairs a little after two o'clock in the afternoon. Hannah would always peek through the slack in the rug to check around. That day, she saw the cat sitting there in front of her. She was surprised to see it and staggered back down the steps. Andrew peeked through the gap between the floor and the rug and saw the cat looking back at him and meowing. Delighted, Andrew jumped out from under the rug with great glee and grabbed the cat.

"Come quick, Hannah, I caught a kitty cat!" Clutching the cat to his chest with one arm, he pulled Hannah out from under the rug with the other.

"Stop that, Andrew, it hurts."

"Come on out here, quick."

"My hair will be frayed on the carpet if you keep pulling me like that." Her hair tousled; Hannah came out of the basement. She stared at the cat.

"Weird."

"What is?"

"Its whiskers are cut off."

Andrew took a good look at the cat's face. "You're right, it doesn't have whiskers. Strange.," he said and handed the cat to his sister. Petting the cat's head, Hannah went running to Mrs. Berger who was in the living room.

"Ah, Hannah, Andrew, you noticed the cat. It's a little skinny, but it's cute, isn't it? It's been here since yesterday, wanting to be friends with you."

"What's its name?"

"It doesn't have a name. I thought I'd leave the naming to Andrew."

"He's tiny and he looks funny, so we can call him Tiny."

"Okay, then we now have two little guys—tiny Andrew and Tiny the cat," Mrs. Berger said.

"I'm not tiny," Andrew protested. "And Tiny has puny whiskers, so we should call him Puny."

Aside from violin practice, it became more fun for Andrew to chase Puny around the house than anything else. Mrs. Berger didn't stop him. It was because Andrew was finally acting like the child that he should have been. Perhaps Puny had a good ear for music, for any time that Andrew would play off-key, Puny would push his ears backward. It amused Andrew, and he would deliberately play jarring notes to see Puny's reaction. Mrs. Berger laughed along at first, but she reprimanded him by the fourth sour note that he made.

"Andrew, doing that will damage your instrument, your ears, and your heart as well, and it'll make you so insensitive that you will start accepting strange sounds. Now, stop it."

Both Andrew and Hannah believed that their strange but enjoyable days would go on forever.

The snowy winter has come to an end. Just as the tulips had finished blooming, they received a word that Mr. Berger would be returning briefly from his concert tour. Once again, they were going to choose pieces to play for another home concert.

Mr. Berger arrived home two days earlier than expected.

"I'm home," he called out, after opening the front door without making a sound. He had wanted to surprise everyone with his early homecoming. In a flash, Puny the cat ran out the open door. Mr. Berger had not known that a cat was living in his home, and he didn't notice what was happening around his feet. He was carrying bags filled with presents and went straight into the kitchen.

His wife was in the midst of preparing lunch. She was so surprised when she turned around and saw her husband standing at the end of the kitchen that she almost dropped the plate that she was holding.

"You're home!"

"Sorry I startled you. I was able to come home earlier than scheduled. Are the children all right?" Mr. Berger examined her face for any sign that things may have changed. She noticed his scrutiny, and deliberately put on an exaggerated expression on her face to tell him that she was well.

"Of course they are. But we haven't finished planning the program for our homecoming concert."

"That's fine, you can do that anytime. I'll join everyone this time."

"Oh, have you seen Puny?"

"Puny?"

She told him about the Siamese cat with the clipped whiskers. "He became part of the family after you left."

"I haven't seen him."

"Puny? Here, Puny. Come and have some milk. Puny—" She called again and again, but there was no answer from Puny.

"Oh, no. He must have gotten out when you came in. Andrew's going to cry."

"I'll go out and look for him."

"Please. I'm sorry, I know you've just gotten home."

Mr. Berger shrugged.

"Mr. Berger!"

It was Andrew who ran up to greet him. Mr. Berger turned to him, picked him up in his arms, and told him how he had grown. Andrew chuckled with the excitement of seeing Mr. Berger again and the sense of freedom in coming upstairs.

"You can't come up here unless I give you the signal." Mrs. Berger scolded Andrew in his innocent merriment.

"But I-I… I heard Mr. Berger's voice."

"Oh, it's all right." He said in Andrew's defense, but his wife was adamant. "Now, go on back to the basement."

Andrew was taken aback, as Mrs. Berger rarely scolded him. He was too young to understand just how dangerous the situation was. But he paled, thinking he may have done something terrible.

It was then that they heard the faint meow of a cat from outside the front door. "Hush," Mr. Berger said. The meowing was coming closer and closer. But something didn't feel right. "Andrew, quick, hide behind the drapes. Don't you dare move!"

No sooner had Mr. Berger said that had they heard an incessant knocking on the door.   "Nazi Secret State Police. Open up!" a voice outside commanded.

Taking a deep breath, Mr. Berger slowly opened the door.

"Hello, Mr. Berger. Is this your cat?" A man in uniform stood outside the door.

"Oh, uh, yes. I was about to go out to look for it. Thank you so much."

The officer was holding the cat by the scruff of its neck, and passed it to Mr. Berger, who plopped it in the arms of his wife who was standing behind him. The officer stood at attention, kicked the heel of his right boot against the left with a sharp click, raised his right hand in a salute, and shouted, "Heil Hitler!" Mr. Berger stood at attention and offered the same salute.

"Mr. Berger, Headquarters has issued an order. You are to report to the Russian front."

The officer handed the papers to Mr. Berger and saluted again, saying, "Heil Hitler!"

It was then that Mrs. Berger relaxed her arms slightly, and in an instant, Puny slipped out of her grasp and ran, of all places, straight to where Andrew's shoes were showing by about an inch from behind the drapes. Puny rubbed itself against Andrew's legs and began to purr.

Trying to act normal, Mrs. Berger stepped back gingerly and tried to pick up the cat.

"You're not hiding anyone, Mrs. Berger, are you?"

"Certainly not."

Mrs. Berger's heart caught in her throat. Her mind began racing as she began wondering if her voice might have cracked or her gestures may have been exaggerated. The Gestapo officer walked straight into the house, pushed her out of the way, and pulled back the drapes to the left. It all happened so quickly, and there was no way for Mr. Berger to have stopped him. Andrew stood there, trembling.

"Oh, Andrew, so that's where you were. No more hide-and-seek," Mrs. Berger spoke in a cheerful voice. She then pulled Andrew in front of the officer. "This is Andrew, my student. Andrew, why don't you play Boccherini's *Minuet* for this gentleman?"

"Ah, he can play the violin? He's still a little boy."

The man appeared to be impressed. Realizing that the man's attention had turned to music, Mrs. Berger thought this was her chance.

"This child is a prodigy. Please do listen to him play a piece before you leave."

Mr. Berger took out his cello and spoke casually to Andrew. "I'll play the cello part, and you, my dear, the second violin. Andrew, take the first violin. This is a chance to show your talent."

Though still a child, Andrew realized that the one piece that he played would determine his fate. He sensed that he was now in grave danger. The Bergers watched anxiously as Andrew bravely picked up his violin.

The officer sat back on the side sofa and rolled in his hand one of the chocolates that were scattered on the table, which resembled Andrew's current situation. If the officer discovered that Andrew was Jewish, it would be solely up to him whether to crush the poor boy or take him away. Mr. Berger signaled with his hand, and the performance began.

The proud performance that Andrew gave was good enough to surprise the man. It may have helped that he was small for his age. He finished playing, held his violin under his left arm, and gave a bow.

"Danke, that was splendid," the Gestapo officer said. He shook Andrew's hand, exchanged handshakes with Mr. and Mrs. Berger, and left.

Seeing the door close, Mrs. Berger sank to the floor. "Quickly, Andrew, go back to the basement." It was all she could manage to say.

But what happened on that day had been but a moment of sheer luck. As soon as she regained her composure, Mrs. Berger remembered her husband's draft notice.

"This is awful. You have to leave tomorrow evening. What are we going to do?" Mr. Berger went into the kitchen and spoke as he made a pot of tea.

"It's okay, there's no need to worry. I'll probably be assigned to the army orchestra, so things won't be that much different. I've always led a good life wherever I've been, and I can't thank this cello enough for that. What I'm capable of doing is giving the gift of music to anyone who longs for it. If doing so instead of praying will give me salvation even for a moment from the crime that my people have been committing, then that should be my duty. Don't worry about me." He reassured her as he poured her a cup of tea.

"Yes, darling, you're right. Even back when you were a prisoner of war in Japan, you were able to make a better time of it than anyone else. I'm sure that God will bless you with a good life this time as well."

Contrary to her words, Mrs. Berger couldn't stop the tears that fell down her cheeks.

7

It felt safer the next day, as the Gestapo had left town. The Janssens were helping with the preparations for the farewell party for Mr. Berger. Grandpa Janssen engaged in conversation with Mr. Berger while two wives prepared the meal. Mr. Janssen, Hannah, and Andrew were in charge of the decorations. It was when Andrew was passing colored paper rings to his father as he stood on a chair to attach it to the ceiling that the front door suddenly burst open.

"Hello, Child Prodigy." It was the officer who had paid them a visit the previous day. Everyone forgot to breathe at the sight of the man in the long black coat. As if attempting to smooth things over, Mr. Berger raised his right hand and saluted, "Heil Hitler!" as he approached the man. "I wasn't scheduled to leave until this evening…"

"Klaus Berger, you are to leave immediately."

"But my friends are about to throw me a going-away party."

"That's too bad—but this is the order. There's also a task that I had forgotten about yesterday," he said as he walked up to Andrew. "You are Andrew Janssen from the neighboring town, aren't you?"

Paralyzed with fear, everyone swallowed hard. They had been pushed into a deadly corner. No one in the room imagined that they could get away from the man who now stood in front of them. As much as they wanted to help little

Andrew, who had suddenly become the focus of attention, no one knew what they could possibly do.

Mrs. Janssen regretted the fact that she hadn't explained to Andrew the reason why he had to live in hiding in the basement in a way that he could understand. She wished she hadn't brought the cat to her home. Mr. Berger regretted not having told his wife when he would be coming home. Grandfather felt powerless, and Hannah bit her lip.

"You are Andrew Janssen, aren't you?" the Gestapo asked again. Andrew, who was on the verge of tears, nodded.

The officer barked an order to the men in three police vehicles that were waiting outside, and they stormed into the house. It was exactly as they planned.

Although Hannah had her violin case slung over her shoulder, Andrew didn't have time to retrieve his small violin, and the Bergers weren't able to take their instruments, either, as they were taken away. They were driven for what must have been more than four hours. The vehicles came to a stop, everyone was brought out, and the two families were put together once again.

It was at 3:43 p.m. on March 28, 1942, that they first set foot on the grounds at Dachau concentration camp. The Bergers were forced to wear the red uniforms of political prisoners, and the members of the Janssen family had numbers tattooed on their arms. Hannah was tattooed with the number D15783 on the inside of her left forearm. She was no longer to be called by her name. She became a number from that point onward.

8

The Bergers alone were subjected to an interrogation. Perhaps because they had been arrested at the scene of the crime of harboring Jews, the interrogation consisted of nothing more than routine questioning to confirm the facts. As Mr. Berger had been an honorary citizen of Germany, he and his wife were granted permission to return to their home. But because the Janssens were

Jewish, they were transferred without question from Dachau to a concentration camp in a faraway town called Oswiecim, south of Warsaw, Poland, known as "Auschwitz." The place would eventually be known as an extermination camp equipped with gas chambers.

Although Mr. Berger wondered briefly what had become of his induction order, he could not very well abandon the Janssens. He asked the director at Dachau, "What will you do with the Janssen family?"

"They will be sent to Auschwitz. It's none of your business, Klaus Berger. You never knew any Janssens." The director spoke monotonously as if he had not a semblance of emotion.

"I'll return home with my wife for now, but I will go to Auschwitz with the Janssens. I can't leave them to die."

"Darling!"

"You wait for me at home."

The director was incredulous that Mr. Berger was asking to be sent to Auschwitz of his own accord and put down the cigar he had been smoking.

"Are you crazy? We can't afford to lose someone like you, the pride of Germany. Please understand, Klaus Berger."

"It's all my fault. I was hiding them."

The director was thunderstruck.

"You are certainly an odd one. We will transfer you to Auschwitz tomorrow. An orchestra will be organized there. You serve as a conductor and keep an eye on the Jews. You will be a guest from Governor-General Hitler, and I don't want to get rough with you."

"But I left my cello at home."

"It will be sent to you, so you needn't worry about that."

Once the director finished speaking, Mr. Berger was grabbed from both sides by SS soldiers and made to sit at the back of a Gestapo vehicle separately from the Janssens.

As for the Janssens, they were ordered while being transported in a convoy to board a train that was bound for Auschwitz. The train was already packed, and they were attacked by a foul stench the moment the car door opened. The odor was so terrible that it was almost impossible to breathe, and Mrs. Janssen vomited outside the door. Several people shoved her out of the way and ran out of the train car, but were immediately shot dead by the SS soldiers. Hannah and Andrew began trembling at the horrific sight.

"Mama!"

Mrs. Janssen clutched Andrew to her chest, covered his eyes, and somehow managed to get on the train. Andrew had wet himself in fear. He was not alone. Several others in the train car had also done the same.

Each train car was equipped with a large container that was to be used as a latrine, but they were already full. And it was so crowded that people could barely manage to stand where they were, let alone reach the containers. Women could hardly be expected to go to the bathroom in the presence of others, and those who were having their periods were pitiful, unable to clean themselves up. It was no time to feel embarrassed. Everyone was forced to remain standing without food or drink for days on end, and some had gone over their physical limits and died in their standing positions. Others collapsed, died, and were being stepped on. But no one had the emotional capacity to feel sorry about the deceased. They were confused and terrified about what was happening and what could possibly be in store for them. All that Mr. Janssen could do was to use his body to shield Hannah and little Andrew from the weights of people around them.

Chapter 3: Hannah

1

In September 1941, Zyklon B, developed by I. G. Farben, was tested on nine hundred Soviet prisoners of war at Auschwitz. The cyanide-based pesticide proved to be effective. It took about ten minutes to kill every captive, and a decision was made to use it in the mass killing of the Jews. The Wannsee Conference of senior Nazi officials was held on January 20, 1942, where an agreement was confirmed to deport Jews to the east for forced labor. They were relocated from Germany and German-occupied areas throughout Europe. The objective was their annihilation, and extermination camps were built at several locations in occupied Poland. Auschwitz-Birkenau was one of them.

No one on that train, including Mr. Janssen, had an inkling of where they were being taken or for what purpose. He felt dizzy. He had just about reached his limit and was losing the strength to hold his children in his arms when he thought he heard the sound of music. It sounded like *Voices of Spring* by Johann Strauss. He wondered if he was finally beginning to hear things from the world beyond when the train car suddenly shook back and forth with a large thud and came to a stop. The passengers were let out.

Andrew and Hannah looked up when they recognized the familiar melody.

"I hear music!"

"It's Strauss!"

Although the music was almost drowned out by all the voices around them, the Janssens, as they set foot at Auschwitz, saw a band performing. Hannah wasn't sure if it was to welcome their arrival, but it gave her a sense of relief.

It was the type of music that gave people hope. Unfortunately, the feeling of relief quickly dissipated.

A commander in uniform and a doctor waited for them on the platform. They made the passengers stand in a single file and asked each person to state their age and the state of their health.

"Andrew Janssen. I'm five," Andrew said in a low voice.

Without a word, the doctor flicked a finger to the left, his demeanor indicating that it was a waste of his time to bother to speak. The commander pulled Andrew into the line on the left. It appeared that his role was to decide which line they would go.

Grandfather was next.

"Farman Janssen, seventy-four. High blood pressure, general malaise…" Grandfather was still speaking when the doctor pointed to the left.

"To the left!" the commander shouted. Grandfather joined the line on the left and grabbed Andrew by the arm.

"Hannah Janssen, fourteen."

The doctor pointed to the right. Hannah, her father, and her mother were placed in the right line, separated from Andrew and grandfather. The people on the left appeared to consist mostly of young children, the elderly, and those who were weak or ill. They were shoved onto transport trucks as the screaming voices of mothers became louder and louder. Mrs. Janssen sensed that something was terribly wrong and ran up to the commander.

"Where are you taking my boy?"

"Mommy, I'm scared! Mommy!"

"Andrew!" Hannah shouted her brother's name as loud as she could.

"We are keeping the children at a nursery," the commander said to Mrs. Janssen. "You will be together again soon."

Grandfather looked at her and nodded as if trying to reassure her. Andrew clung to his arm, looking desperately at his mother like he was about to burst out crying. There were children on the truck who were much younger than Andrew, crying and screaming, and a young mother whose infant had been taken from her was kneeling on the ground, wailing, as if she had lost her mind.

Several freight trucks arrived at the scene, and one after another, the people in the left line were forced to board. Babies were tossed into the vehicles as if they were pieces of cargo. The process was soon completed, and the convoy left for Block 11 outside the barbed wire fencing that surrounded the camp.

The newly arrived had no idea where their families were taken. Their uncertainty was somewhat appeased by the cheerful music that was being carried by the wind, much like a spider's thread that led to hope. The truckloads of people were dead within thirty minutes. They became a part of the dull, gray smoke that rose into the dark sky that loomed over Auschwitz. The process was nothing more than an everyday routine at Auschwitz, similar to a process at a factory where goods are placed on a conveyer belt and seen to matter-of-factly. By the time the smoke overhead had started to thin out, it was time for the next group to arrive. There was never a day in Auschwitz when the skies above were clear.

2

Hannah and her parents believed that they would soon be reunited with Grandfather and little Andrew. There was a roll call for the younger, healthier group, and then they proceeded to enter the gate. A sign was put up at the entrance that read, "Work Brings Freedom," but it didn't take long before they realized otherwise. The barbed wire enclosed a site where about two dozen two-story wooden barracks and stone buildings stood in rows.

Before the prisoners were assigned to their quarters, an orchestra of captives in formal attire began gathering at the camp entrance. They played cheerful numbers and German folk songs as the new arrivals saw laborers returning from a day of hard labor, dragging their feet and looking utterly exhausted. Some collapsed as they walked through the gate, never to awake again, which was a frightening indication of what laid ahead.

Hannah's mother was assigned to Block 5, and her father was sent to Block 4. It was Hannah's turn to be told where to go when she was approached by a female captive who had been standing by Hitler's Schutzstaffel, or SS soldier.

"That's a violin you're carrying, isn't it?" she asked.

"Huh?"

Hannah had forgotten that her violin case was still strapped around her back. Although everyone had been told to leave all their belongings in a certain spot when they got off the train, no one had told her to remove the case on her back. It had gone unnoticed, which could only be described as a blessing for Hannah.

"I'm Arles Bizet. Don't be scared, I'm Jewish, too."

Hannah thought she was beautiful. Her red lips were a bright contrast against her long, straight black hair, and she reminded Hannah of an elegant rose. There was also an air about her that seemed to say that any attempt to touch her would mean being pricked by her thorns. Arles Bizet may have been a prisoner, but she was a dignified noblewoman.

"Do you play the violin? How well can you play?" The woman asked Hannah questions in rapid-fire succession.

"We will leave D15783 to you, Arles," the SS soldier watching over her said. Hannah noticed that Arles wasn't referred to by her number. Hannah later learned that Arles was a violinist who was very famous throughout Europe and that Hitler had kept track of her movements to ensure that she was not sent to the gas chamber. Because Arles had been using her husband's surname, she had slipped out of the Drancy internment camp in France and ended up at Auschwitz. To make matters worse, they had initially put her in Block 10, where medical experiments were being conducted. The plan had been to make Arles pregnant, remove the fetus, and to use its organs for experiments. But one day, a female doctor was looking for music to celebrate her upcoming birthday, and Arles volunteered. She was promoted as the leader of an orchestra that was to be formed at the female camp and had since been receiving special treatment.

Hannah had never met anyone like her. Physically, Arles was just another detained Jew at Auschwitz, but mentally, her spirit continued to exist on a higher plane. No matter how difficult the conditions around her became, she focused solely on the world of music and would have never descended until the day she died. Hannah followed Arles and stepped away from the group of prisoners.

"I took lessons from Mr. and Mrs. Berger for almost ten years," she said in a low voice. "I can't play Vitali's *Chaconne* yet, but I've practiced a lot of other pieces."

"You mean, Klaus Berger?" Arles exclaimed in surprise. "I can't believe it. Finally, I have a decent musician! What's your name?"

"Hannah Janssen. I'm fourteen.

"Hannah, can you play Schubert's *Ave Maria*? All the Germans here want to hear it. Play it for me?"

Hannah opened the case that was strapped around her back and started tuning her violin. She told herself to keep her calm, recalling how Mr. Berger had taught her to put her heart into all her performances, wherever she might be. Though there was no question about the fact that she had become a prisoner at a horrible concentration camp, she had to be composed in order to appreciate, and deliver, the joys of music. Hannah took a deep breath and concentrated on the pleasures that the sounds brought her. She played her violin with all her heart. After listening to a few passages, Arles told Hannah to stop.

"That was amazing. I'm so glad you're here, Hannah. You don't need to play the whole piece; I can tell that you're the perfect person to be my right-hand man—or rather, right-hand girl. Commander, I'll be responsible for her," Arles declared to the commander who was watching her.

"You want her in your orchestra?"

"Yes. I believe there's a vacant room in the special block. Put her there."

"You're a lucky one," he said to Hannah. "Live and perform well."

The commander appeared satisfied and stepped away. That was when Hannah realized that she had left the queue.

"Where's my mother? And my father?"

"They are in the block for laborers. Listen to me, Hannah. It's very important here that you can play music. It means you've gotten yourself a ticket to live."

"What happens in the block for laborers?"

"It's…harsh." Arles didn't elaborate. Hannah recalled the glimpse that she had gotten of the laborers when she was getting off the train. Emaciated with empty eyes, some were dragging by the shoulder those who had become too weak to walk, some of whom had already perished. Hannah was not too young to understand what life in the laborers' block meant.

3

The commander told his superiors about Hannah, and before she knew it, she became a major topic of discussion. People soon came up with a number of descriptions for her:

The girl who was praised by Arles Bizet.

The young violinist who enchants people in a brief, impromptu performance.

A blue-eyed beauty of a violinist in Auschwitz.

Arles took her to the music room made of brick and introduced her to the nine members of her orchestra, telling them that starting the next day, Hannah would join their rehearsals as a top member. There was a stir among the members, a sense of anxiety that could not be expressed in words, and Hannah realized then that she was not quite welcomed. Arles didn't appear to take note of her discomfort and handed her a dress.

"Wear this. Come here right after the roll call tomorrow morning. We usually start around six. Okay?"

"…Y-yes, ma'am."

"The commander will take you to your room. I have to practice now, so you go on and get some rest."

Hannah remembered that she had had nothing to eat or drink, not that she was hungry. It was probably due to the tension. She stepped outside the brick building and was taken by an SS man to a block some distance away. She thought Arles had said that her quarters were right in front of the music room, but as she had no knowledge about the camp, she had no choice but to follow the guard.

She was taken to the laborers' block a good distance away, where she was thrown onto a bed in a room that was partitioned like a chicken coop. The bed was a crude fixture in a wooden barrack, and there was only one blanket for every three people. It was Hannah's first day at Auschwitz-Birkenau, separated from everyone in her family. She was scared, sad, lonely, and miserable, and unable to get any sleep that night. They were issued only one set of thin prisoner clothes. Many people developed scabies, and the sound of itchy skin being scratched echoed through the night.

Hannah was finally starting to doze off when an SS guard came and told her that Arles Bizet was looking for her. It was too early for the morning roll call. The prisoner who had been sleeping in the bunk next to hers suddenly turned toward her. "Are you a member of Arles Bizet's orchestra?"

"Uh, I don't know much about her orchestra, but she told me to come to practice today."

As soon as Hannah had spoken, the woman in the upper bunk in front of her jumped to her feet.

"You…Nazi dog!"

She spat at Hannah. Fortunately, she missed her face, but the sheer act was just shocking. Hannah had never met such hostility in her life. She didn't even know this woman. Having no idea how she could have made her so angry, she simply sat there, unable to speak.

"Stop it," said the woman in the bunk next to hers. She handed Hannah a handkerchief and spoke to the other woman. "Don't cause trouble in a place like this. It's uncalled for."

But this woman wasn't friendly, either. She averted Hannah's helpless eyes. "As for you, girl, just go. Go to your practice or wherever you were told."

Hannah realized that she was an outcast. Maybe it wasn't her. Maybe they hated the orchestra. But either way, it made no difference to her. A thought crossed her mind that perhaps it wasn't that they hated the orchestra so much as wanting to become a part of it. But the thought didn't stay for long.

With no better understanding of what exactly this orchestra meant to everyone, Hannah left in a hurry and headed to the block where Arles Bizet awaited. She stepped inside the section in the brick building that was called the music room and saw Arles standing there, screaming at the people around her.

"Hannah, you're late! Did you forget about our early morning practice? I told you that we were assembling at six!"

Hannah wondered how she was supposed to be able to make it at six when she had no watch. Still, she saw that the nine other members had already started their practice and were barely paying attention to her.

"I'm sorry, Arles, I couldn't sleep last night…"

"You aren't in the block for laborers, are you?"

"I don't know. I ran three blocks to get here. I'm in a wooden barrack with no windows."

"I told that SS guard where to put you! Oh, I suppose the communication didn't get as far as the other guards. Look, Hannah, your room is at the end of the brick block in front of this music room. It's a private room, and you even have a real bed. There's a desk, too, and you get special meals. Now, change out of that prison uniform and put on the clothes I gave you yesterday."

The other members appeared to be afraid of Arles and her direct and somewhat high-handed manner. It didn't bother Hannah, though, and she felt better when she changed into the white blouse and long navy-blue skirt.

"We must always be properly dressed," Arles said when she returned, satisfaction apparent in her expression. We're now working on *Radetzky March*. Come here and join our practice." Arles was waving her baton in front of the nine members when she suddenly stopped and snapped the stick. Sighing, she turned to Hannah.

"You can see what I meant when I said I needed your help. Everyone here is relatively new at this, it's only been two or three years since they first held a violin in their hands. They have the basics covered, but can't make decent music yet. We can barely follow the scores. The orchestra will be disbanded if we don't master at least three pieces in the next two weeks. Do you know what will happen then? The gas chamber. Either that or hard labor. Either way, we'll be done for. I get sick with worry wondering what to do when we can barely play a single piece."

"A single piece...?"

Hannah could now see the gravity of the situation. No wonder Arles was so picky about being on time for practice!

There were four members in the first violin section, another four on second violins, and one on the viola. Hannah was given the task of training the first violins. She played one note at a time for Marie with pretty freckles, who seemed to have no idea how to read a score. A faint smile appeared on the girl's face when she was able to produce the notes that Hannah taught her.

"I'm next," she said.

"Huh?"

"Next in line to be kicked out of the orchestra."

"What?"

Marie explained that only a limited number of members were allowed to play in the orchestra, and Hannah's arrival had already led to the departure of someone who had been sent to the laborers' block. Arles had been delighted to have Hannah join her orchestra. It was obvious that the conductor saw her as her savior. But it also meant that someone else had to leave. Hannah couldn't blame the members for not being welcoming.

"I know I'm useless as a musician, and I'm always nervous, wondering what I'm going to do if there's someone among the new arrivals who can play music," Marie told her. "I have to admit that I wasn't happy when I heard you'd joined the orchestra, but that was terrible of me. I'm sorry, Hannah—"

Hannah shook her head. She had only recently arrived at the camp and was clueless as to the pressure that Marie had been under. She was the one who wanted to apologize.

"Let's polish your skills so you can play well. There might be new arrivals who can play instruments, but you should focus on improving so you'll be better than them. I'll coach you so you can pick up the skills quickly. Feel free to ask me any questions, any time."

"Thanks. I'll practice harder."

They started early in the morning, and by noon, Marie was able to play long-phrases completely in line with the others. Arles looked overwhelmed with happiness and took Hannah's hands into her own. There was a change in the attitudes of the other members as well. They realized that Hannah's arrival would help them instead of threatening their existence, and the mood improved. They also looked forward to the added benefit of not having to worry about Arles' hysterics. Practice in the music room became joyous sessions.

Being a professional with high standards, Arles was very demanding. But because Arles and her orchestra were recognized by the SS officers, they could ask for improvements in their daily living conditions, including food and other supplies. The members knew that they were much better off than the other prisoners who slaved away at their labor all day long, and for that reason, no one harbored resentment toward her.

4

"Help!"

It was toward the end of practice that the screaming voice of a woman was heard outside the building. "Someone please, help…!"

Arles, Hannah, and several other members of the orchestra ran outside to see a woman from the laborers' block came rushing toward them. Her face was devoid of color and her lips were trembling. Right before Arles started running toward the distraught woman, she turned around and held up a hand.

"Not you, Hannah! Go back to the music room!"

Having only recently arrived at the camp, Hannah didn't understand why Arles was telling her to stay behind. She tried her best to keep up with the orchestra leader. Arles did not want to show her the things that were happening at this camp, but there was no time to explain. She knew that time was of the essence.

Arles soon arrived at a tense situation where a midwife and a woman cradling her newborn baby in her arms were surrounded by three SS guards. The baby had been born a few minutes earlier.

"Cover its mouth."

"No!"

"Then give it to me!"

The mother wept and held her baby tighter. The midwife stood bravely in front of the mother and the baby as if to shield them.

"You can't take the baby away! She's our hope!" She spread her arms widely as if to indicate that she wasn't afraid to put her life on the line for them.

"Excuse me." Arles pushed her way through the crowd gathered at the scene. She steadied her breath and stepped in front of one of the guards. "Hold on there a minute! Are you going to take the life of an innocent newborn baby?"

"You know how things are, Arles," he said. "There is no milk to feed babies. You do understand—even if we let this one live for a while, it will be a sad life."

"You don't know that!"

"It would starve because its mother can't nurse. Isn't it better to end now before it starts to see and feel?" The guards were willing to reason with Arles because they respected her for her musical talent. Just for an instant, she was taken aback by the reality of their words.

And then it happened. Another guard shot the baby, along with its mother and the midwife.

"Hans! How could you…?"

Arles knew the ruthless man by name. She stared at him with disbelief.

"I'm just doing my job," he said. "I've wasted two bullets."

"What—"

She was about to reproach him when something hit her face. It was a ball of mud. "You don't have the right to say anything, Nazi dog!"

"Get out of here! We don't want your pity!"

"You're just feeling superior, thinking that you're saving us, helpless prisoners!"

One by one, the people who had been watching in the crowd began attacking Arles. They were all prisoners; all Jews. Just like her. Yet they lashed out at her and flung mud at her beautiful face.

"Get out of here!"

"Go back to your own block where you have a comfy bed and a change of clothes!"

As the shouts continued, Arles bit her lip without saying another word. She clenched her fists, her nails digging into her skin, and her knuckles pale. Arles had come to help them, and her fellow Jews ended up attacking her, making her feel lost. She lowered her head and left the scene. People were killed, and they took it out on Arles. It was an everyday occurrence at the camp. She wasn't as flustered by the things that had happened at the previous camp she had been in, and she learned to cope when she was treated unfairly. But she had yet to get used to the pain.

Hannah was hiding behind others and witnessed what had just happened. Only two days after her arrival, the young girl now understood why no one wanted to talk about the camp and the fact that the orchestra members were indeed receiving special treatment.

5

Hannah was told to sit next to Arles starting from the second day of practice. She was given a private room, and there were even curtains for the windows. Other than the fact that she was often hungry and constantly being watched, it sank in that she was living in a completely different world from the other prisoners. She thought about her family. Is Andrew okay? How was Grandfather's back pain? Was her father worried about her?

I want my mother.

The tears began to fall.

Why does something like this have to happen? How long would I and my family have to endure this terrible situation? There is no school here. What am I supposed to do in the future? How is my grandmother? Why did my beloved sister have to die?

How she craved a taste of fresh-baked bread. Some cheese. A bowl of steaming soup. Her sobs became louder.

"Oh, Hannah—"

Arles had heard her and stepped into the room. She gently pulled her up from the bed and softly patted her back. "You're too young to have to go through this. Let me tell you something, Hannah. Music will save you. Let's work together, okay? The situation isn't going to go on forever. Do you have siblings? You don't look like an only child to me."

That triggered another burst of tears, and Hannah began to cry louder.

"My sister was killed. My brother Andrew—was told to get in line on the left-hand side with grandfather. They said they were taking him to a nursery school, but…" she was unable to continue.

Arles didn't know what to say. It was all she could do to pray that Hannah would not hear from anyone that neither her little brother nor her grandfather survived.

"Take a deep breath, Hannah, and get some sleep. We have an early practice tomorrow morning." She pulled the cover over Hannah's shaking body and watched her till she fell asleep. It didn't take long. She must have been exhausted. Arles gently pulled the golden hair that was plastered against Hanna's face from the tears and quietly left the room.

6

It was the fifth day since Hannah had joined the orchestra, and they were finally able to play *Radetzky March*. They had to master two more pieces in the next ten days and began practicing Schubert's *Military March*, which was fortunately much easier than Radetzky. It took them no time to learn the main melody, and they spent the afternoon practicing *Edelweiss*. Marie could read scores by the time the orchestra learned to play *Radetzky March*, and was moving her bow with much more finesse.

As musical scores were not easy to come by at Auschwitz, Arles would sit down after practice to write scores from memory, write arrangements, and divide up the sections for an ensemble. She often negotiated with the members of the male orchestra, hoping that they would agree to come and join the women's practices. There were also occasions when the kapo, fellow prisoners who had been chosen by the SS guards to carry out some of their duties, called on the musicians to perform at their birthday events and such. Assembling an all-female orchestra at Auschwitz was no easy task, and it ensured that Arles was kept extremely busy.

Marie practiced late each night so she wouldn't cause trouble for Arles or the other members of the orchestra. One day as they were about to start general practice for the third piece, she collapsed with a fever. Fortunately, it was not a typhoid fever. Arles made a deal with the female doctor, promising that the orchestra would play at her birthday the following month if she could give Marie as much medical attention as she possibly could.

Arles was stepping into the rehearsal room for the male orchestra, hoping to ask a cellist for his help, and stopped in her tracks. She couldn't believe who she saw conducting the orchestra.

"Oh, my goodness, Klaus Berger? Is it really you?"

"Arles! I'm so glad to see that you're okay."

Klaus and Arles had performed together many times during their youth and had mutual respect for their talents.

"What are you doing here, Klaus? You have no business being here."

"Don't you have a girl by the name of Hannah Janssen in your orchestra?"

"Yes, I do—oh." Her expression brightened. Hannah had said she'd been taking lessons from Klaus.

"Hannah told me. You taught her well; she's my trusted right-hand person now."

"I give my wife most of the credit."

Arles nodded, recalling meeting his wife in the past. "How is she?"

"She's at home, taking things easy. She has students to give lessons to and can manage on her own. I have nothing to worry about."

"But what are you doing here?" Arles couldn't figure out why the German musician was here at the concentration camp.

"We were hiding the Janssens in our home. We were initially sent to Dachau, but my wife and I were released when they recognized me from my previous performances at the military headquarters and other facilities. I found out that they had transferred the Janssens here and asked the head person at Dachau to send me here to be near them. They were like my family, Arles. I couldn't just leave them here to die."

"I see. I didn't know there were still 'good' Germans around." She was being sarcastic. She was there because she'd been persecuted by Germans, like everyone else at Auschwitz. It was hard to imagine that any German would want to go through the trouble to help a Jew.

"Politics created a dangerous society, but individually, the Germans are good people. I'm not the only German who's been captured, you know."

"Are you kidding? It's you Germans who've been supporting the regime. How many Jews do you think have been killed? You probably don't know that not a single day goes by when you don't see the smoke rising from the four crematoriums here."

To Arles, Klaus's words sounded like nothing more than a feeble attempt at whitewashing what was happening. Although she was well aware that Klaus himself was a fine individual, she couldn't help being lashing out at him, just for being a German.

"You're right, things are terribly rotten. I realized what was happening after I came here. To survive this place, you have to become numb so you can be oblivious to the things that are going on, or else you'll go mad."

"I've stopped trying to figure out how music can exist in a place like this. Instead, I've found that a pure pursuit of the world of music can be my sole purpose to live."

"That sounds just like you, Arles. You seem to know what it is that you ought to do through music. I came here hoping to find a way to save the Janssens through my music…"

Arles could see the determination and a sense of justice in her old friend's eyes and wondered if she should tell him what she knew about Hannah's family. She concluded that it was pointless to hide the facts.

"Only Hannah and her parents are still alive."

"What?"

"Please don't tell Hannah, but her younger brother and her grandfather were sent straight to the gas chamber."

In a grim voice, Arles told Klaus what she had heard from Hannah about her arrival at Auschwitz, and what the separation of her family meant.

"I see." Klaus bit his lip. "It's—it's beyond words. I don't know what to say."

"It's a holocaust. We, the children of God, are being sacrificed in the place of animals. Why do we have to be the ones? What have we done to deserve this? Why isn't God putting a stop to it? What is this, Klaus?" Arles began to cry. Since arriving in Auschwitz, it was the first time that she had let her guard down. She had endured hardships and humiliations and had somehow managed to maintain her composure by immersing herself in her music.

Klaus pulled her into his arms and gently patted her back.

"Listen to me, Arles. You have your music, the almighty God of the universe."

Music. The word brought Arles back to her senses. She took a step back and ran her hand through her disheveled hair.

"I'm sorry—I don't know what came over me." It took only a moment for Arles to bring back her usual self—a woman who suppressed all her emotions.

"Don't worry about it. Hey, didn't you come here for something?"

"Oh, yes, that's right. I wanted to borrow a cellist from your orchestra. We're finally starting our performances tomorrow, but we're still missing something in our lower notes..."

"I'd be glad to help out. Any time."

Klaus was a cellist, and he graciously volunteered to play with her orchestra.

"Really? You wouldn't mind performing with us? But how about your own orchestra?"

"I have an idea. I'll introduce you to a handsome Polish man I've been coaching here by the name of Leo Rochester. He can perform with you whenever I can't make it."

"Thank you, that would be great. Could you come to our music room this afternoon?"   "Sure, I'll bring Leo with me. What should we practice before we join you?"

"*Radetzky March*, *Military March*, and *Edelweiss*."

"Not a problem. We'll be able to perform those pieces right away."

7

This was the day when Arles decided to have faith in God. It was true that her hopes had been crushed too many times. But once more, she wanted to forget about those times and simply believe in Him. No matter how hopeless her present condition may have been, she had a strong desire to live. That was why she couldn't help believing—hoping—for divine intervention. Her unexpected encounter with Klaus was like finding God's will in this hell on earth.

Klaus and Leo visited the women's orchestra room that afternoon. Klaus immediately spotted Hannah, who had lost weight and appeared to have shrunken in size.

"Hannah!"

Hannah turned at the sound of the familiar voice, unable to believe what he heard.

"M--Mr. Berger?" She clutched the violin that Klaus had given her in her left hand and jumped into his arms.

"I'm glad to see that you, Hannah."

"Did they send you here, Mr. Berger? Because of my family?"

"No, no, I volunteered. I wanted to be here so I could be with you."

"What about Mrs. Berger?"

"She's fine, Hannah, there's no need to worry about her. She's keeping her house tidy, waiting for you and your family to come home."

Leo stood next to the teacher-student duo and smiled at the exchange. He thought of his late parents and the loving family that he had once been a part of. Hannah reminded him of his younger sister, who had also died, which made him feel instantly close to her.

Arles was watching on with tenderness in her eyes. After giving them a moment to catch up, she turned to the other members and offered an introduction to the cellist.

"This is Klaus Berger, the famous leader of the Berger Ensemble, and this is Leo. He's, uh—"

"Leo Rochester, eighteen," the younger man with the straight black hair offered. "Good afternoon, ladies."

Leo's eyes were deep green, and he said he was part Italian. His smile was like a breath of fresh air, and for just a moment, he made the women in the room forget that they were in this terrible concentration camp. Hannah suddenly remembered that she hadn't been able to take a shower for days. She was self-conscious about her limp hair and dandruff, and embarrassed that she probably smelled, too, and attempted to hide behind Klaus, but he didn't seem to notice. He pushed her in front of Leo and introduced them.

"Leo, this is Hannah, the child prodigy I was telling you about. I know you two will get along wonderfully."

Leo took Hannah's right hand and kissed it. She quickly pulled it back, stunned to have someone kiss it for the first time in her life. Amused by the girl's shyness, the orchestra members roared in delight. Arles clapped her hands twice and called for attention.

"All right, everyone, let's get to work. We're having our first performance tomorrow."

As expected, Klaus played beautifully, and the practice ended in thirty minutes. He suggested to Arles that the men and women's orchestras practice together starting with their next piece and that way, they would become a real orchestra rather than two separate ensembles. But Arles didn't respond, as she had always believed that music was best played by an ensemble.

8

The following day was for the women's ensemble to make its debut. The members were assembled at the camp gate at six in the morning. They played *Radetzky March*, *Military March*, and *Edelweiss* as people began trudging to their forced labor. They had virtually locked themselves up in their music room for their intense practices, and it had never occurred to Hannah to think about why they were rehearsing with such fervor. Arles was very demanding, and it was all that Hannah could do to focus on playing as best she could. There was no room to wonder why they had to play these pieces, the meaning of their performance, or who exactly they were supposed to be playing for.

It wasn't just once or twice that passersby heading for work would stop and spit at the performers. They were denounced as Nazi dogs, and it reminded Hannah of the morning of her arrival when she had been shocked by the outrage that was directed at her. She watched another group drag themselves by and suddenly stopped playing her violin. These people are nothing but skin and bone. They were pushing their limits, and it was obvious that it took great effort to reach their destination, even before the day had begun. Of course, they'd be angry to see the comfortable life that the performers had. They were all prisoners at the same concentration camp, but their differences were like heaven and hell.

Hannah couldn't blame them for their rage at the women's orchestra. It embarrassed her to think that only a few days earlier, she had wondered if the people in the laborers' block might want to become a part of the ensemble. How would she have felt if she had been one of them? She, too, would have despised the musicians, hated them for the security that only they got to enjoy.

Klaus noticed that Hannah had stopped playing her violin and shook his head. "Try not to look at them," he said softly. Hannah nodded and caught up with the performance.

As the last row of prisoners marched by, Hannah glimpsed a familiar face in the crowd. A woman who was coughing—followed by a man who seemed to be watching over her. Her parents. She should have been happy to see that they were alive. But the emotion that overcame her was a grave concern. Her mother, who had always been healthy, was coughing uncontrollably and appeared utterly exhausted.

Hannah couldn't remember the last time her mother had been sick. She wanted to call out to them: *I'm right here, Mother! Father!* She must catch her parents' attention now. She raised her violin, drew the bow high, and shook it left and right in exaggerated movements. Mr. Janssen looked up and noticed his daughter's face and leaned over to whisper something to his wife. Mrs. Janssen raised her head. The husband and wife turned toward the violin section. Their eyes finally met.

"Hannah! Oh, Hannah!" They extended their arms. Mrs. Janssen coughed again choked. She was very sick but mustered her strength to call her daughter's name. Mr. Janssen was wearing a huge smile on his face. A moment of happiness came to Hannah. She was overwhelmed with emotions when she noticed that an SS soldier was running toward her parents with an iron bar in his hand. It was Hans, who had killed a newborn infant, its mother, and her midwife without a second thought. Hannah later learned that it was one of his duties to kill laborers who had become weak and therefore was feared as "Hans the Murderer," the crazed man who was bored with the simple method of using a gun and preferred to pound his victims with an iron bar until they stopped moving.

"Mr. Hans, no! Those are my parents!"

The laborers were well aware that they couldn't afford to look sick in front of Hans; his attention meant death. It was up to him to decide when and how a sick prisoner would be finished. Despite their frail condition, the prisoners suppressed their coughs and smeared red clay on their faces to give the impression that they were well.

Hannah ran to her parents as fast as she could. "Mr. Hans!"

"What?"

Hans turned around. He was a monster whose favorite pastime was interrupted. The violent glare in his eyes made it clear that he was ready to crush whoever dared to get in his way.

"Hannah, go back!" Mrs. Janssen shouted with all her strength. Mr. Janssen waved his arms in the air, frantically trying to stop her from coming to their rescue.

"Stay back!".

"It's my fault! I shouldn't have tried to get you to notice me. Please, Mr. Hans, don't hurt my parents!" Hannah ran up to Hans and surprised him by planting her feet in front of the huge boulder of a man. He was aware of the girl's reputation. The trembling, skinny girl was known as a child prodigy and strikingly beautiful. She spread out her arms and took a bold step forward, ready to be stricken if he so desired.

The scrawny girl was nothing. Hans certainly didn't need an iron bar to harm her. But despite her shaking body, the fierce look in her eyes made him lose momentum. It wasn't as if he had been moved by the love that was apparent between the child and her parents. It simply didn't amuse him to crush the girl to pieces at this point. He clucked his tongue.

"You little bitch. Don't ever get in my way again." He waved the iron bar a few times to indicate that he wouldn't be so nice next time, its swooshing sound reaching her ears in a threatening way.

Hannah ran to her parents and hugged them tightly. The danger seemed to have passed, and she fell into her mother's arms, her father wrapping his arms around the two of them. She couldn't help noticing that her mother's body seemed to have shrunken, but she was overwhelmed with joy. She was finally able to find comfort in the cocoon of her parents' love that she had been yearning for for so long.

Hans made it clear that he was not moved by such a display of family bonds. He swung his iron bar again and shouted. "I'm only letting you go this time on account of your daughter. Now get going! Don't disrupt the line!"

As Mr. and Mrs. Janssen resumed their procession, they were hit in the legs with clubs. The kapos, fellow detainees who had the role of overseeing their fellow prisoners, were there to make sure that the prisoner march continued.

"Mother! Father!" Hannah continued to call out to her parents long after they were out of sight. The distance was unbearable, not being able to be with them while knowing that they were nearby.

It turned out to be the last time Hannah saw her parents.

9

Because evening performances at the gate were handled by the male orchestra, Hannah had no way of knowing if her parents made it back to the camp that evening. Klaus and Leo were there. They saw stretchers being hauled in. There were ten bodies and the bloody, broken body of a woman whose head had been cracked open, and a male body with a bullet hole through the chest. It was Mr. and Mrs. Janssen. Klaus recognized the bodies and froze. He ran over to the kapo at the end of the line and grabbed him by the collar.

"What have you done to the Janssens!?"

"I don't know any Janssens. We go by number."

"How can you say that? You're a Jew just like everyone else! I'm talking about the body of a woman!" Klaus punched the kapo hard. It wasn't enough. He jumped on the man, pulled him to the ground, and grabbed him by the collar again, stunning the orchestra performers with his sudden outburst. Klaus was a big man, but always had a gentle soul and rarely raised his voice.

"Okay, okay," the kapo croaked. "Let go of me and I'll tell you. The SS soldiers are coming, so I'm going to make it quick," he said, rubbing his neck. "She was coughing and had a fever these last few days—pneumonia, I bet. Should have gone to the medic but we all know the docs decide who gets gassed. So she chose to work."

The kapo spoke rapidly, fearing that the SS soldiers might not approve that he had stopped to talk to Klaus. He said Mrs. Janssen's cough had become so violent that the others around her told her to stop spreading the disease, which eventually led to a mass attack. Hans the Murderer came to the scene so fast and used his iron bar on everyone involved.

"A guy tried to snatch the bar. Her husband, I think. He was shot by another SS and fell on top of her. I'm a victim too, you know. Hans blamed me and punched me," the kapo said, rubbing his swollen cheek with his hand as he turned around and ran inside the gate.

Klaus fell to his knees. He pulled at his hair and sobbed. This couldn't be happening. He had hoped that he would come here and somehow manage to rescue the Janssens, but he had been powerless. Had he been arrogant to think that he could save anybody's life just because he was a German? He told himself that he was not responsible for the Janssens' death. It had been caused by their involvement in a scuffle between the prisoners. But he felt utterly helpless and the only way he could go on was to face this tragedy, acknowledge that he was a part of it, and live the rest of his life in their honor.

Hannah became the sole survivor of her family.

10

Too many terrible incidents happened around Klaus. There was a man named Kelly who played the flute. He had been imprisoned at Auschwitz along with his wife and his mother and one day was allowed to join the orchestra. He was moved to the musicians' block, after which the whereabouts of his family became unknown. Despite his worries, he was a cheerful man who often told jokes and never complained about personal issues to the people around him. Everyone respected him for his resilience and was impressed by his ability to tell jokes when life at the camp was hard and no more than a step away from death.

It happened during practice one day. It was a rare, clear day. For once, there was no smoke in the sky. Kelly was playing his flute beautifully in determination to perform well, while three transport trucks rumbled past the orchestra. As the third truck rolled past them, Kelly thought he heard a familiar voice and raised his head. He couldn't make out what the voice was saying but knew that it was coming from the vehicle, a muffled moan amid the heartbreaking cries of many.

Shocked, Kelly paused his flute. He focused on the direction where the voice was coming from and suddenly saw an arm that looked like a dried-up twig stretched out toward the orchestra. It belonged to his seventy-year-old mother. He would have heard her cries if he hadn't been playing his flute, he thought at that moment. The music drowned her voice. It was only when the truck came directly in front of him that he finally heard her. Kelly wondered if his focus on his music made his own, dying mother's suffering even worse.

Until then, he prided in his music. But how good could music be if it were a part of evil deeds? For a brief moment, Kelly felt numb. Then he realized what was happening and ran after the truck.

"Wait! It's my mother! Please, slow down!"

"Kelly...oh, my son!"

He couldn't keep up with the truck. It was soon out of sight, and he could no longer hear his mother's voice.

Kelly tripped over a rock and fell. He didn't have the energy to get back up. In his mind, he left his mother to die. He had wanted to maintain his dignity by performing well, and for that, he had sacrificed the woman who had brought him into this world. He could never forgive himself. Even if everyone in the world told him otherwise, he knew that he could never justify the fact that he was performing for Nazis.

That day changed Kelly. His energy drained out. He barely spoke and became an empty shell. Klaus, as the conductor, had a responsibility to watch over every member including Kelly, but there was nothing he could do to ease the grief. He could only leave him be.

Another tragic incident occurred three days later. Achel Cohen, a vocalist in the orchestra, was found in his room bleeding from his mouth, unresponsive.

Achel was a rabbi, a spiritual leader, a counselor, and an educator in the Jewish community. He was a wonderful, reliable person that had a presence over his congregation. Jacob, a trumpet player, had gone to see Achel a week before.

"The Nazis cut off my right hand," Jacob had lamented, carefully showing his bandaged wrist with his left hand to indicate what was no longer there. "They loaded my friends onto a boat and made it explode, as an experiment. They were laughing and boasting about the bomb. I couldn't help it, I punched one of the SS soldiers with my right fist. So they slashed it off at the wrist."

Achel looked at Jacob with tenderness in his eyes. A calmness came over Jacob. Jacob had visited other rabbis many times for different reasons in the past but could not remember ever receiving such unconditional love.

"You were fortunate, Jacob. Things may have been difficult if you were on other types of instruments, but with the trumpet, you can learn to use your left hand. Everything will be all right. Perhaps you were meant to lose your right hand when the time comes to cross the lake of fire, but you have now been set free. God protects you."

It made sense to Jacob. He used to have a habit of stealing, and a lot of times he didn't even realize that his hand had done the deed. He had never been so poor that he had to steal in order to live and had not stolen expensive items— only petty things like cigarettes, fountain pens, combs, and umbrellas. He would often realize what he had done, and then slap his right hand with remorse. The rabbi's words brought Jacob a sense of relief. He would no longer need to worry about this bad habit. He was now relieved that the right hand was gone.

But the rabbi himself was facing his own demon. He had seen the members of his synagogue put to forced labor, and witnessed them perish one by one. Achel would come across them at the camp and have fingers pointed at him, anger and hatred burning in their eyes. "You abandoned us to save your own life!"

The proud leader of the Jewish faith was crushed. Their words, and enormous guilt, tormented him so badly that on that fateful day, he bit his tongue and bled to death. One of the former members of his congregation in the laborers' block later told Klaus about the incident. He wanted to convey to the conductor the despair Achel had to endure.

Klaus believed the rabbi to be a strong, level-headed individual. He had no inkling that the security that the orchestra gave its members had been such a burden on Achel.

First, it was Kelly, and then the rabbi was gone. Klaus could not help blaming himself for his inability to prevent the tragedies. And Hannah's parents had now been murdered.

Everyone in the orchestra knew that Hannah saw her parents. They were unaware of what had happened to them after the brief reunion and could not help but smile as they shared the joy.

"I'm so happy for you, Hannah. You'll be able to see them every day now," Edie said, rejoicing as if it were her own.

"I'm going to practice hard so mother and father will be proud of me. Oh, and guess what? Mother plays the piano."

"Then you should hurry up and tell Arles about it. You'll be able to save her!"

"Arles told me that when I first came here... I guess she's been busy and forgot about it. I'd better mention it to her again. How about your parents, Edie?"

It was the first time that Hannah asked Edie about her family.

"My father...was a lawyer, and my mother was a doctor. They both worked, and I was basically raised by our nanny. We were ready to leave for Switzerland when the hunt for Jews began. We were unlucky. We had just finished packing most of our valuables when the Nazis found us. They took our bags. We fought them. We needed those bags to survive. And...my mother...and my father...they were both killed on the spot. I don't want to talk about it anymore."

"Oh, Edie... I'm so sorry."

"It's okay, Hannah. Your parents are still alive, so you should take care of them. This place is filled with so much sorrow—we need to find happiness wherever we can. Otherwise, it's impossible to go on."

11

That afternoon, the female orchestra was told to visit a crematorium less than a mile away from their barracks.

The trains continued to arrive several times a day. People used to be divided into two lines, one for labor and the other, the gas chamber, in an orderly fashion. The new arrivals who were put in the latter group had no idea what was to become of them. The orchestra played such cheerful, welcoming music that it made people wonder if it wasn't such a bad place they'd been brought to after all. Music was used as a tool of deception.

Soon after, the SS guards stopped dividing up the new arrivals and sent everyone to the gas chambers. And when the chambers were overfilled with bodies, they threw young children into the incinerators alive. Their screams could be heard at distant barracks. To drown out the sounds of their cries and to cover the unthinkable acts being carried out, the orchestra was ordered to play music.

They were not permitted to play requiems for the dead. There was nothing that they could do but close their eyes tightly when they heard the screams of unbearable agony that sometimes drifted in the wind. They had no choice but to carry on with their music. Otherwise, they knew, the same fate awaited them even with a mere act of covering their ears.

Hannah began to see the brutal reality of what was going on at Auschwitz, and because she could not stop the shaking in her legs, she went off-key no matter how hard she tried to concentrate. Edie, on the second violin, could not bear the sounds nor the smell. She vomited in between performances.

One night, Arles called a meeting in the music room. They went over the schedule for the next day and were told which pieces they were to perform.

"Things went quite well today, considering that it was our first time. I know that there are a lot of disturbing things going on, but please, try not to get distracted. Just play. Focus on making the best music that you possibly can."

Edie shook her head. "This is too much! I can't bear it! I'm quitting. Hard labor is better than this! Who are we playing for? What's the purpose? Someone, please tell me!"

No one could give her an answer. They had all been feeling the same way.

"Then go ahead and leave," Arles said in a cold voice.

Not expecting such harsh words from the leader, Edie took a step back and stared at Arles.

"It isn't just to you, Edie. If it's too horrible for you to be here, then go on, move to the laborers' block tomorrow. A lot of people would love to be sitting here if you're willing to offer them your seat. They have barely anything to eat, they're all skin and bones, and they're forced to work ten hours a day in the extreme weather. If that's what you'd rather have, then go ahead, you can leave right now."

Edie swallowed hard. So did the other members of the orchestra. Edie had not been the only one who was beginning to think that it would be easier to work, no matter how tough the conditions might be, compared to sending off their fellow prisoners to their deaths. But they had food there, however insufficient the amount seemed to be, and had decent clothes. They even had private rooms. It was heaven compared to the laborers' block where they were given soups that were not much more than slightly salted water, where they had to wear the same, flimsy prison uniforms day in and day out, and had to sleep in crowded barracks that were better described as stables. Giving up the arrangement here meant torment and death.

Arles sat next to the younger woman and gently placed her hand on her back.

"What you've just said is something we all have been asking ourselves," she said in a low voice. "Do you think I'm numb to it? Let me tell you something. I've felt exactly the same way as you have, for a year now, but I've persevered. Now you listen carefully."

No one said a word. Arles glanced around at all the faces. This time, she touched Edie's hair.

"I know I sounded harsh. I want you to continue to play music and survive. There isn't a single person at Auschwitz who wishes to die, right? We mustn't let their deaths be meaningless. We've got to live through this and tell the world about this holocaust. One of these days, Soviet troops or the British military will come to free us. Until that happens, we have to persevere. We have to stay alive."

Arles spoke with determination. She gave the impression that it was their responsibility to live through the holocaust, not only for the sake of their own survival. Fate had brought them to the orchestra, and they were destined to survive.

"You all know about Kelly, the man who played the flute in the men's orchestra? He barely speaks these days and seems to have immersed himself in his music. That's not unusual. What happened to him can happen to any of us. Listen, although we're just like any other prisoners out there, we will not be rounded up for hard labor that almost guarantees death. As long as we continue to play music, we'll be given access to food, and we'll be allowed to dress properly for our performances. Hannah, have you ever thought about where our supply comes from?"

Hannah had no idea. Despite being in a concentration camp that lacked everything, she had been given a decent outfit from the time that she first joined the orchestra. She had never given too much thought, but it did seem odd now.

"Everything that we're given had once belonged to someone who died, down to the soap you use and your pillow, if you were given one. They are made from the hair and fat of the dead."

Hannah gasped. So did Edie and everyone else. They quickly covered their mouths with their hands.

"You see, quite simply, we're no better than those dreaded kapos. We earn favor from those Nazi bastards and watch our compatriots die. It isn't that we're happy to see them die, but other people see it that way." Rosa, a woman on the first violin with Hannah, opened her mouth.

"I made up my mind some time ago as to why I perform," she said. "It's to offer a moment of comfort—however brief that might be—to the people who get off the trains. It's for them in the barracks when we're playing by the crematoria. When we play at the gate, it's to cheer people on when they go to work, so they can find the strength to come back alive. And when we play there in the evening, it's to welcome back the exhausted people who've endured another hard day of labor."

Arles continued. "We brainwash the Nazis into believing that they can't live without our music, and to cleanse the hearts of kapos of the crimes they're committing by controlling our compatriots."

Edie nodded.

"And we play for our own good."

Hannah wanted to add that it was also for everyone's parents, then swallowed the words, remembering that some of them no longer had theirs.

"That's the spirit, ladies," Arles said as she stood up and opened her arms.

"Stay positive. Think deeply about the world of music if you want to escape. I will not allow you to choose otherwise. See you all back here at six o'clock tomorrow morning."

12

Hannah had taken a step out of the music room when she remembered something important. She turned around and looked at Arles.

"I saw my mother and my father this morning."

She had to ask Arles to allow her mother to join the orchestra.

"Oh, yes, that's right. That Hans—I'm going to punch him good one of these days! Were your parents all right?"

"Uh-huh. Um, Arles? About my mother…"

"Oh, I'm so sorry, it had slipped my mind completely, what with so much happening every day. I'll go and see the manager tomorrow and tell him that we want your mother to join the orchestra. And while we're at it, I think your father could manage the flute. Let me talk to Klaus."

Hannah was delighted. Maybe she would soon be together with her parents again. It would be a dream come true.

"Arles. Hannah. That…isn't going to happen…"

It was Klaus. He was standing outside in the darkness. Arles turned to him and said slowly.

"What do you mean?"

Klaus pulled Hannah in his arms and squeezed her tight. His voice shook as he tried to speak. "Your parents…I'm sorry, they're no longer—"

Klaus was not able to continue, but the agony in his voice conveyed the message. Hannah pushed him away as hard as she could.

"No… No! You're lying, Mr. Berger! I saw my mother just this morning!"

"Your parents…there was an incident at work, and unfortunately, they were involved. I'm so sorry, Hannah."

"No! That's not true!"

Klaus grabbed Hannah's hand as she continued to step back. Perhaps she thought she might be able to turn back the hands of time if she retreated. He pulled her into his arms again and held her. She cried hysterically. Huge drops of tears fell from Klaus's face to the top of Hanna's head as well, and they were not the only ones who were weeping. Arles, Edie and Rosa, who had been on their way back to the room, and everyone else in the orchestra stood in a tight circle around the two. The sound of their cries seemed to rise higher than the smoke that spewed from the chimneys at the crematoria.

Klaus reached into his pocket and pulled out a crinkled up piece of paper.

"I have something for you, Hannah."

It was a letter from her mother.

"Your mother had been clutching this in her hand."

Hannah wiped the tears off and took the piece of paper from Klaus. She carefully stretched out the creases so she wouldn't tear it.

May 1, 1943

My Dear Hannah

I hope you aren't hungry. I hope you're sleeping okay on your own. I hope you aren't sick. I hope you aren't crying from loneliness. I hope someone's being kind to you.

I worry about you and Andrew every day. I go to sleep each night praying that I will see you in the morning.

I can't begin to tell you how glad I am that you learned to play the violin. I heard a rumor about a girl who joined the orchestra. It has to be you. I sometimes hear the music in the distance. It gives me energy when I think

that you are a part of it.

Your father is alright. I pray that we will soon be back together, living the way used to. Until then, I will persevere. I will not get sick. I will not die. Whatever happens, let us dream about tomorrow and survive. Don't you ever give up, my child. Remember, I will always be watching over you.

I have been fortunate enough to find a pen and some paper. I am writing to you whenever I can. Hide my letters inside your violin or somewhere where they won't be found.

Your loving mother

Hannah read the letter and wept. Her mother had been worried about her. But wasn't she the one who must have been hungry? How she must have suffered, terribly ill, yet was forced to work under the freezing cold weather. It was too late to worry about her now, but Hannah couldn't erase the image of her beloved mother, shrunken to skin and bone. It was only that morning. The vision had been etched into her mind forever.

"Your parents were wonderful, loving people," Klaus whispered gently as a kaleidoscope of images rushed through Hannah's mind: eating bread at the Berger home without realizing that her mother gave her some of her rations. The bedtime stories that her mother had read until she and Andrew fell asleep. The strong, kind man that her father had been. Their beautiful smiles. They were gone forever. She would never see them ever again.

Clutching the letter in her hand, Hannah sobbed in Mr. Berger's arms. She continued to cry until her throat hurt.

13

The following day, Arles came to Hannah's room before practice.

"I don't want to force you, Hannah, but this is a crucial time for you. Don't try to make sense of things, because nothing does anymore. Just play your music. I know you can."

She stepped inside and saw Hannah lay face down on her bed. "Come on, everyone's waiting for you. We need you so we can stay alive. You have to survive for your family. You're their legacy. Come on now."

Hannah did not move. She pulled away when Arles tried to grab her by the hand. Arles pushed her shoulder and pulled her up, and slapped her.

"You need to grow up! You aren't the only one who's had a tragedy. I know how you feel, and I know you don't believe that you could possibly play music again. But Rosa and Marie, who's still terribly sick—they've lost their families, too. Music is what's keeping us alive. Imagine how much those who perished had wished to keep on living. Think about those laborers. Things are so tough for them that they wonder if it would be simpler just to give up and die. But you know what? They lift their heads and do their best to go on. I don't believe that you're incapable of feeling how they feel. Come on, Hannah, come to practice. Perform and give courage to someone who's struggling out there."

Arles picked up the violin that leaned next to the bed and tuned the A string. She cocked her head slightly and tried again, and then moved on to the E string.

"This is strange. The slight reverb—it sounds like an echo. It sounds completely different from the way it did yesterday…"

Hannah jumped up on the bed.

"It might be because of my mother's letter I put inside through the F-hole yesterday. It was moving around inside so much and I didn't want it to fall out, I was tapping on the chinrest with my hand and then it got stuck inside, and now I can't pull it back out."

Arles smiled. "You're probably right. Your mother's letter is like a wall inside that creates a faint echo. It's a wonderful sound that you will never get with another violin."

Arles started to play *Ave Maria*. Sure enough, the sounds were deeper and had a richer quality.

"Your mother is watching over you, Hannah. She's showing herself to you in the form of music."

Hannah nodded. She hugged her violin to her chest as she would her mother and a smile slowly appeared on her face.

Someone knocked.

"Arles? Hannah? We're going to be late for practice. Let's go."

It was Leo, the cello player. He felt terrible for Hannah and stopped by to see how she was doing. He led the women outside, acting cheerfully as if all were well with the world. Hannah and Arles looked at each other.

He was relieved to see the smile on them.

Arles picked up her pace so Leo and Hannah would be walking side by side. Despite the harsh circumstances, she thought the two were a good match. How wonderful it would be if Leo could give Hannah some emotional support she so badly needed.

Hannah walked a step behind Leo so he would not get a clear view of her swollen eyes. But he suddenly turned around and put his arm around her shoulder.

"You're going to turn into a chameleon if you cry too much."

"That's not nice, Mr. Rochester," she said, hiding her face with her violin.

"It's too late for that, Miss Chameleon. And you should call me Leo."

She discovered then that the cool texture of the violin was perfect for soothing her puffy eyes. From that time on, she always cooled her eyes with her violin after she wept.

Hannah smiled when the other members greeted her warmly at practice. Though circumstances were almost unbearable, the orchestra gave her strength. Her peers gave her the courage to go on. Klaus winked to Leo. Arles saw the exchange and smiled.

"Okay, everyone. This is the beginning of the Bizet-Berger orchestra."

14

Hannah became Arles' right-hand girl, and she immersed herself in her music. As she did, she learned to cope with the harsh reality of what was going on around her. She tried to imagine that she was watching a film. She learned to close her mind when she saw the emaciated bodies of her fellow Jews as they headed to work. She focused instead on each performance that she gave, and her techniques continued to improve dramatically. Hannah would stay up late going over the performances that they had given during the day and help Arles write scores, working hard so she would not have time to think about anything else. She was often summoned by the SS soldiers to play her violin to mark special occasions. Although such ties with the SS would help a prisoner win their favor and improve their chances of survival, the fourteen-year-old musician was terrified of entertaining the Nazi soldiers alone. One day, she worked up her courage and made a gentle suggestion to an SS man.

"I think I could perform better if I had someone accompany me with lower notes…"

"Perhaps so," came the reply. "The cellists—it would be Berger or Rochester. Bring one of them next time."

Hannah did a cartwheel in her mind and thanked the SS. And from then on, her tension-filled solo performances became something to look forward to. It wasn't extremely nerve-racking to perform for the soldiers if she was there with another musician. They were occasionally given better food to eat, and more than anything, she was desperate to give superb performances so the Nazis would feel a need for the orchestra to continue to exist.

The sounds that this beautiful blond, blue-eyed girl created on her violin gradually began to capture the hearts of the Nazi SS soldiers. Even Hans, the cruel demon himself, quieted down like a kitten when he listened to Hannah's performances.

One day, the SS soldiers were discussing a situation that they now faced. There were too many bodies to move from the gas chamber to the crematoria. There were at least a hundred more bodies to process that day, and the incinerators were overflowing.

Hans sneered. "I have an idea." He thought he had to be a genius. It was an excellent solution. "About a hundred more today, right? No problem."

"I hope you aren't going to do suggest something evil again," a comrade said.

"Something evil? There's no good or evil here at Auschwitz!"

"God may be good to us now, Hans, but there's a limit to what He would allow us to do. I sometimes get sick of the extent of your brutality. You're headed straight to hell, you know that?"

"Me? What're you talking about? If I'm going down, then so are you. Are you telling me that you're doing this with compassion? Ha! There's no such thing. We'd be just murdering robots at an assembly line if we can't think of fun ways to finish them off."

Hans was excited to try his own idea. First, he made the prisoners strip out of their clothes and dig a long, deep ditch. Then he made them line up with their backs facing the ditch and had a few SS soldiers stand guard. He aimed and fired from left to right. The prisoners fell into the ditch like a stack of mannequins, a hundred lives instantly gone. The other SS soldiers were expressionless as they took part in the killing. But Hans, who was proud of his shooting skills, started humming an up-tempo *Ave Maria* as he expertly shot his victims between their eyes.

Even to his fellow SS soldiers, Hans was a heartless demon. Some of them averted their eyes, knowing that those prisoners had children and families, but Hans appeared to have no qualms about shooting each of his targets, who ranged in size and height. He laughed. "Take that, you filthy Jews!"

"Hey, Hans."

"What?"

"Will you stop humming *Ave Maria*? It's blasphemous."

"Who's greater, me or Jesus? Look at my amazing skills!"

"Okay, okay. Just stop your humming, will you?"

Not far from the ditch, Hans had another group of prisoners carry bricks to a spot 600 yards ahead and then bring them right back to where they had started. He had also made a group of them dig a hole in the morning and then fill it in the afternoon. Forced to repeat such same meaningless actions, the prisoners began to lose their minds. Hans kept close watch over them and then suddenly barked an order.

"Jump into the barbed wire!"

The prisoners raised their voices and ran to the fence as fast as they could, instantly got electrocuted.

The idea had come from a conversation that Hans once had with a doctor who told about the effects of meaningless repetitions. It proved to be very entertaining for him.

One night, the other SS soldiers were feeling sick of Hans's actions and summoned Hannah and Leo to the bar to play music. For Hannah and Leo, t had become their routine to give special performances for soldiers and officers as a duo. *Ave Maria* was banned from public performances with the orchestra, but the soldiers requested it nonetheless. It quieted the monsters. Some even listened with tears in their eyes.

Even Hans seemed like a human being. He closed his eyes to listen, then spoke in a gentle voice like a soft, warm blanket.

"You play it in such a special way, Hannah…"

His colleagues agreed.

"It washes away our soul," one colleague said, with his eyes red. "Especially you, Hans."

Hannah was expecting Hans to explode. But he didn't. He was surprisingly calm. What did he consider to be his sin? Weren't the SS soldiers abusing the Jews because they wanted to? She wished she could ask the soldiers if they were aware of what they were doing to other human beings. She wanted to ask them why.

It was on this day that Hannah thought she felt a sense of sorrow among the Germans. She spoke to Leo about it on their way home and found that he sensed the same thing.

"There's something that I've come to understand since we began performing together," he said. "Those ogres seem to crave for music. At first, I thought it was a mere cultural thing, but I'm not so sure anymore. I don't know how to describe it, but if they're still human in any way, they must need music to cling to a small piece of humanity. Do you know what I mean?"

Hannah nodded. "They're like werewolves who are desperately clutching onto their humanity so a full moon wouldn't turn them into wolves."

"Exactly. I don't think they are complete monsters, but politics is making them werewolves. You agree, don't you?"

Hannah thought about Klaus. He was a good German. Even some of the SS soldiers were nice when they listened to her music and gave her things in return. She was no longer sure if hating the Germans for the rest of her life as she had earlier vowed was justified.

Leo and Hannah talked about a lot of things. They talked about the schools that they used to attend, their old friends, and the emotions that they were now experiencing, and they became inseparable. They both knew that without each other, they would not be able to find the strength to go on at this concentration camp.

Intermezzo: The Children of Brahma

1

One evening, Klaus asked his orchestra members a question. "Did you know that there are people in this world whom we describe as 'the children of Brahma'?"

"Brahma?" Hannah asked, wondering what the unfamiliar word might mean. "Yes, the children of Brahma. It's an old Indian term that refers to a celestial world—their idea of heaven. It's how an American poet named Walt Whitman once described a group of Japanese samurais when they went to New York to research how to rebuild their country."

Arles sat up straight in her chair. "Do you think heaven exists?"

Klaus smiled. "Let me tell you a story."

The thirty-four members of the orchestra pulled up their chairs and sat around the conductor. They waited for him to take a long sip from the flask of whiskey he'd gotten from an SS soldier.

"My wife and I got married about thirty years ago. There was a war going on at the time—World War One—and I was fighting for Germany. I was posted at our base in Qingdao Island in China. In September 1914, we were surrounded by Japanese troops and taken to their Bando prisoner-of-war camp in Japan—it's called Naruto now, located in a prefecture called Tokushima. Germany and Japan are allies now but were enemies back then. About a thousand German POWs were kept at the camp until around 1920."

The orchestra members frowned at the mention of a camp. They hadn't known that Klaus had been in one, and a facility operated by enemies had to mean the prisoners were used as slaves. Merely imagining the treatment that he must have received frightened them.

"Mr. Berger, you were a prisoner then, just like us."

"I was, yes. So you see, I've been through this before."

"In Japan?" Arles asked.

"Japan is a small country in the Far East, right by China. The Pacific Ocean is to its east, and beyond that is the American continent." Klaus used a fallen branch to draw a map on the ground. Rosa tilted her head. "Where's Germany?" Klaus continued to expand his diagram and pointed to the area he had just drawn. "We're over here."

The musicians squealed in surprise. Japan was at the edge of the world. "You were all the way out there?" Klaus nodded and poured more whiskey into his glass. Arles wasn't the only one who was eager to hear more. Everyone wanted to know about Klaus's time at a POW camp. Knowing that Auschwitz was a living hell, they were curious about how he managed to survive.

"Go on, Klaus, tell us about it."

"There were rows of barracks at the camp there, like we have here. The biggest difference was that they didn't have gas chambers or crematoriums. Yes, those were the days…"

2

The strong rays of the sun seared my face relentlessly. The single-story wooden building was surrounded by the imposing presence of armed Japanese soldiers. It didn't look likely that there was any way to escape. The glare of the sun was stronger than I would have imagined in this place called Japan, and although I was drenched with sweat, perhaps it was my extremely nervous state that made me unconcerned about the heat.

I first realized how hot it was when the gate to the camp appeared before us. I looked up at the sun and I thought I caught a whiff of the sea. This was it. I had been brought to an underdeveloped land of barbarians. I was only eighteen. I may have had guns in my possession, but had yet to kill a single human being. From the gaps between the enemy soldiers, I could see the natives who had come to get a glimpse of us. We were their prisoners of war. Even the dazzling sun above was without mercy. Suddenly, my knees buckled, and I fell face-first on the ground.

I regained my consciousness and understood that I was being half-carried by two people, my feet dragged along the dirt below. I could hear the murmurs of the savages in the distance and no longer cared what was going to happen to me. After a while, someone suddenly kicked me and made me roll over. I was lying on my back when cold water was splashed on my face. I was shocked back to consciousness, shook my head, and heard the sound of laughter. It was the Japanese soldiers around me. It would have been something to be angry about, but I was still young and too stunned to take any type of attitude.

Someone yelled something from behind those men. There was no more laughter. I saw that their faces had turned pale, and although I did not understand the language, I received the impression that the new arrival was not shouting at me but instead reprimanding these two clowns. He then stepped close to me, crouched, put his left hand behind my back, and helped me sit up. His uniform was decorated with many medals, and there was a black mustache above his mouth.

He was a military officer. Was he actually worried about me? He gave me water and proceeded to slip his arm beneath mine and pulled me to my feet. Though my legs were wobbly, I slowly rose and saw him smile. It was beyond my comprehension. I wondered briefly if he was mocking me, but he didn't seem to be hostile. A military man smiling to the enemy? It was a mystery to me.

We walked through the gates at Bando, and I was taken to a square where German soldiers were made to stand in line. Young men in sailor hats, privates and officers from the army and navy, civilian volunteers—it was a mix of all types of soldiers with an array of uniforms that ranged from white, khaki, and marine blue to olive green. The Japanese with the mustache stood in front of the group and saluted, which prompted his compatriot soldiers in the front row to follow suit. First that smile, and now the salute—it was the first time that I had ever witnessed anyone saluting the enemy. What in the world were these people trying to do?

Mustache man began to give a speech. It looked as if he was the one in charge. The German POWs weren't the only ones who were listening. Japanese soldiers, as well as the locals who had gathered outside the gate, all stood at attention and watched the mustache man.

"These men have fought for their country, exhausted their every available means, and become prisoners here at Bando. We are all in war, and we can well understand their predicament. Citizens, do not needlessly stare at or belittle these men. Do not shame them."

Everything was translated simultaneously by a lieutenant named Takagi, who spoke German. The prisoners looked at each other in disbelief. Were we hearing it right? Did this man just tell everyone not to shame us?

Mustache man saw our puzzled faces and smiled. I watched him closely but could see no signs of ill intent.

The local savages, dressed in strange robes that I later learned were called kimonos, began to leave after the chief finished his speech.

After roll call, we were sent to a room where we were examined by a military doctor. I don't believe that there was anything wrong with me but perhaps because I was skinny, the doctor said something to the soldier who was standing next to him.

We were fed after our medical checkup. Rice, vegetables simmered in broth, and a stir-fry of chicken and potatoes. It didn't appear that there was reason to be concerned about what the barbarians would feed us. It was simple but unexpectedly decent. After our meal, a number of us who were thin and malnourished were also given half a sweet potato each. It was delicious.

Then we were put to work. We were handed hoes and told to dig, after which to pour sand into the holes and hammer in solid wooden bars. This is it, I had thought at the time. They were making us dig platforms where we would be killed. I was wrong, though. We were making horizontal bars for exercises.

Mustache man seemed to be saying something about a sound mind in a sound body. From the very beginning, our time at the POW camp was filled with surprises.

3

We proceeded to work the mountainous land within the camp and planted potatoes and other vegetables. We were also instructed to take care of pigs, cows, and chickens, and initially believed that we were being used as labor. I can't begin to describe the joy we felt when we later realized that it had been to sustain us.

We grew wheat, ground it into flour, stored it in bags, and took it to the bakery facility that we built ourselves. Several German soldiers baked bread. It smelled wonderful and brought back memories of home. All the vegetables, meats, and bread that we made ended up on our tables. Provisions may have been modest, but we had fine meals that were rich in nutrients. Eating food that we had made with our own hands allowed us to remember our appreciation to God for the blessings of nature that He provided for us.

One day, I noticed that two Japanese children were standing outside the barbed wire watching us. They followed the delicious aroma of the bread that we were baking. David, our baker, stopped the process and picked up a loaf that he had just taken out of the oven and tore it in half. He was a grumpy man who never smiled. With his usual frown, he went over to the children and stuck the bread through an opening in the fence. Whether it was David's frown that scared them or they were simply afraid of foreigners in general, I didn't blame them for taking a step back, but slowly and timidly, they were drawn to the warm aroma of the bread. They looked at David, then at the bread, then from the bread to David. They were clearly interested but afraid to put out their hands. Mr. Grumpy tore off small pieces and shoved them out to the children. Then he brought his hand to his mouth and acted like he was chewing. No longer able to resist, the children took careful bites. Their eyes widened. They devoured the soft, warm bread without a word.

The children then bowed to David, waved good-bye, and took off. As David watched them, the bright red sunset reflected his profile. Though the corners of his mouth were still turned down in his signature frown, it was clear that he was satisfied. A while later, the manager made arrangements to start selling David's bread to the locals, but that wasn't all we sold. We sold livestock products, our home-grown vegetables, and we even started giving music lessons. A third of the proceeds were used for the operation of the camp, a fifth as our health insurance and the remaining was ours to spend as we wished. It was only at Bando that any type of health insurance system existed in Japan at the time. Thanks to the system, the prisoners were able to receive good medical care at no cost.

The bread that David baked became wildly popular among the people in the community, and they would form queues at the gate when it was time for his goods to start coming out of the oven. We wrapped the bread in papers as you might expect at any bakery shop. There was only one Japanese soldier standing guard at the bakery. But since all he did was stand there and watch, we barely noticed that we were being monitored. Sales were better than steady, and when the higher-ups realized this, they allowed us to open shop right outside the gate.

One day, two solemn-faced young men who had come to buy bread were trying to speak with one of our German soldiers. I watched the exchange from a distance and saw that they were soon joined by another soldier, and they began to walk away in the direction of the manager's office. A short while later, someone came for David. I later heard that the two men were aspiring to become bakers themselves. They soon began apprenticing under David. It was the beginning of cultural exchange between the Japanese and us Germans.

Though everyone had been awkward at first, David was patient. He used a lot of gestures to teach the men how to let the dough rest before kneading. They were young, conscientious, and quick learners. It didn't take them long to learn to speak German while in turn, David also picked up some Japanese. The solemn baker had been tense at first, but his smiles became genuine as they continued to work together. There was a bright light in his eyes, and he was laughing out loud from the bottom of his stomach.

4

I had received my music training since early childhood, dreaming about someday becoming a first-rate cellist. For me, winning meant everything. Music hadn't been much more than a tool to me, and it didn't create many wonderful memories. In fact, I had often wanted to stay away from music forever.

But an orchestra was going to be formed at the POW camp, and it was taken for granted that I would be a part of it. The problem was, there was no cello available. We were in the Far East and western instruments were not readily available, so I decided to make one myself. I began by shaving a log, using long strings, and opening up the f-holes. It was interesting to learn that my home-made cello really did make sounds like a genuine cello.

As we continued to rehearse, Matsue, the manager with the mustache, arranged to have a piano, an organ, and a number of cellos, violins, violas, and trumpets delivered from the Port of Kobe. I immediately took the measurements of a cello, Engel measured a violin, and we got busy making instruments with Paul, our craftsman of violins, while we called on other men to join our orchestra. Not to be too fussy with the sounds that could be produced, we managed to make a large number of instruments that would suffice, considering the circumstances. Paul took time to make one particular violin. It was clearly top-of-the-line, packed with his wishes that the state of peace he had found in Bando would spread on to other parts of the world as well.

Although we didn't have decent tools to work with, his hands seemed to remember the feel of these instruments. He continued to work and the time came to put on the final touches. It was a challenge to find a good varnish. It is crucial since it affects the sounds of the instruments. Paul, unfortunately, caught the Spanish flu and died at the camp. It was at his deathbed that Paul gave me his violin. Years later, when we were liberated from the camp, I took it to a shop in Stuttgart where it was carefully polished and given a Cremona varnish. It was unveiled under Paul's name in 1924.

I hadn't known that Paul had done something else to the violin. He had engraved onto the peg the initials "D", "B", and "L" that stood for "das beste leben"*—"the best life".*

5

"This is the start of Engel's Orchestra!"

The instruments were ready, and Engel announced the start of practice. They began with Schubert's "Die Forelle". *The uplifting song was the perfect piece to play at Bando, a quaint place surrounded by rivers and mountains. We were as lively as trout swimming in a river. I realized for the first time how much pleasure there was in playing music with my peers. I was glad that I hadn't quit playing the cello. The fourth movement is particularly well known in* Die Forelle, *a five-movement piano sonata, and the lyrics are often sung. Though we had set up a choir at Bando, I was appointed to perform the solo.*

Our practices were well under way, and the children in the neighborhood assembled outside the barbed wire fence and listened. They ran away when we approached them, but always came back the following day. Eventually, several of them started bringing empty cardboard boxes with them, which we could see had long bamboo pieces attached on the end. It appeared that the children tried to make their versions of our violins!

It didn't take them long to learn the lyrics. They would sing along, occasionally glancing our way. A chubby little boy seemed to be the leader of the group. He played the conductor's role and used his bamboo stick to point out the errors that the young performers made, his plump stomach swaying with his movements. It was interesting to watch these youngsters, and we shifted over to a spot where we could get a better view of them.

Days went by, and Manager Matsue asked us to teach the children to play instruments. I started giving cello lessons to two of them. Since we didn't have small violins, we had to make them. It turned out to be an unforgettable experience for everyone involved. We all jumped in joy when the strings were set and we played our child-sized instruments for the first time. Parents were showing up and peeking in at the gate, concerned that their children had become so immersed that they were getting home late. Manager Matsue assured them that the kids were fine, and that was that.

Our guitarist Dan taught five children. I helped him build more guitars and in turn, he taught me how to play the instrument. "I never dreamed that I would be making guitars all the way out here in the Far East, let alone become a POW," he said. "Guitars are my passion. Not war."

I nodded.

"And on top of that, I'm even giving lessons. Life is strange."

"I couldn't agree more," said Engel, our expert violinist. "Compared to music pupils in Germany, children here are dedicated. They don't take music for granted. Think about it, someday, these children whom we're now teaching may become the foundation for western music to thrive in this part of the world. I get goosebumps just thinking about the important mission that we've apparently been handed."

Manager Matsue with the distinct mustache sometimes dropped by to see how the music lessons were going.

"This is marvelous. If only everyone in the world could respect each other like this, there would be no more useless wars... Engel, would you come up with some ways to expand our musical initiatives to a greater scale?"

"I have an idea, sir," Engel quickly responded. "Why don't we have a cultural exchange event? Thanks to you, we've been able to play music. Thanks to your procurement of instruments, the Molto Licht Mandolin Orchestra, Engel's Orchestra, the Janssen Choir, and many other players are thriving, and thanks to you, we're teaching the children in the community to play. We'd like to learn more about the traditional culture of Japan, too."

"That's a brilliant idea, Engel. We could use the grounds at a shrine and do something there."

After that, the letterpress printers became busy. Its staff of three prisoners began printing flyers for a cultural festival.

6

On the day of the festival, there was not a cloud in the sky. Matsue stood in front of the crowd and began to speak.

"Ladies and gentlemen, our long-awaited cultural festival will now begin. More than six months have passed since we first received our guests from Germany. During that time, we have come into contact with each other's culture and gained great insights. We have nurtured friendships with the common understanding that people are the same wherever they may be from, and we hope that our cultural exchange will serve as a foundation for peace. I would like to thank each and every one of you for coming and would like to invite you to take part in this memorable day."

Lieutenant Takagi translated for us.

"We have been blessed with fine weather today," Matsue continued. "Let us free ourselves under this blue sky from foolish ideas of conflicts and build peace together. For more than a thousand years, there has been an old custom here on this island of Shikoku to unconditionally accept strangers, the unfortunate, and even those who have committed crimes. We call this our hospitality at its finest. Let us cheer on this memorable day the start of a new era where our thoughts for one another unite as one."

The German soldiers applauded for the Japanese, and the Japanese reciprocated.

We began to play Schubert's "**Die Forelle**" *and Johann Strauss'* **Waltz**. *It was the first time for most of the people in our audience to listen to western music or an orchestra, and they were immediately enchanted. I was starting to be concerned that people didn't need to listen with such serious looks on their faces. I wished they would express joy with* the light-hearted music more casually. When the performance ended, I saw some young ladies rising from their seats. They were geishas, female entertainers.

"Such beautiful music!" one of them exclaimed and started to clap cheerfully. The audience followed suit. Everyone was smiling. The tremendous applause seemed to go on forever. Matsue came to shake hands with each member of the orchestra. It was the moment I realized that music was the ultimate universal language that united people across language and border. Although there had been many times in the past when I had wanted to quit playing the cello, this significant moment made me truly glad that I hadn't.

The world is made up of different countries and different ideas. History has been, and continues to be, a repetition of forced battles for the sake of national interests. It may continue to be the same way in the future. Considering the history of wars and conflicts, the small yet peaceful world we created on that day was nothing short of a miracle. We got to actually experience that miracle.

We began to believe that through the gratitude that we were feeling for creating this wonderful experience and by sharing each other's culture, this miracle that occurred in the Far East could be repeated in all parts of the world. But on the other hand, it may have been something that only remains as a fond memory. Worse yet, the miracle may become nothing more than a brief chapter in the history of the world, and perhaps it would eventually be forgotten.

God showed us peace. We felt that if we could tell others about our experiences and continue to repeat the miracle, then the whole world would be at peace. I hoped that I would someday be able to digest what I had experienced in the Far East. I wanted to understand how true music thrived during that war, and I wanted to put it to use wherever I would later be moving on to.

I rehearsed with my peers each day—incredible, considering how much I used to hate the mere idea of playing music—and performed countless pieces, striving to create a world of sound I was eager to express. By then, the number of members in our prison orchestra had increased to sixty. Those with cooking skills held cooking classes, academic lectures were given, and Japanese and German classes became highly popular.

The camp was filled with cheerful laughter, and although Germany and Japan may have been at war, we formed deep ties as human beings. Our days became more meaningful than ever. The locals, we discovered, were not barbarians at all.

Had God only created a place like this in one location on our planet? This was the ultimate Jerusalem. We had created a tiny utopia in this land in the Far East. There was meaning to everything that we did, and we had made the best of our individual skills. I was proud of my music and quietly thanked my parents for giving me the lessons.

7

The war eventually ended, an armistice was signed, and the German Empire collapsed. A notice arrived that we were to be set free. I was happy and terribly sad at the same time. A sergeant among the prisoners suggested that we play Beethoven's **Symphony No. 9** *as an expression of our gratitude to the people of Japan. Since we had connected with the locals in the deep part of our soul, he believed that it would be the most suitable piece to play one last time before our departure. Everyone was in complete agreement.*

"Wait a minute, we need a mixed chorus," Janssen said. "We'd have to rewrite the whole piece if our all-male choir's going to be doing the singing. I'm not sure if we have enough time for that…"

He was right. Rewriting an entire arrangement for all the instruments entailed an enormous amount of work, not to mention arranging the parts for the choir. But we didn't want to leave this place with any regret. We wanted to perform **the Ninth.**

"Okay, then, let's check the vocals in the choir," the sergeant said to Janssen. "We'll see what their highest key is, and we'll go from there. We'll split the writing between us. There isn't much time left, so we need to get cracking."

"I was thinking the same thing," Janssen replied. "All right, let's get right to it.

It's a male solo and a mixed chorus of sopranos, altos, tenors, and bass, so our issue will be how to handle the female soprano part. We don't have any castratos among us and we have to check out the altos—yeah, we'll probably need to rewrite everything."

Janssen went to the choir and told them of the decision to perform Beethoven's Symphony No. 9 as their final performance. Engle watched as he divided them according to their part. "Wegner, Stephan, Flesch, Koch, you do the solos. We don't have sopranos, and we have five altos…I guess we'll need to lower the key by half an octave…"

"Yes, rather than cutting down the number of performers to match the altos, we should have as many of our members take part as possible. But we don't have time to rewrite the whole score."

Janssen looked at Engel. "You're right, we don't. We can leave the tenor and bass as they are and change the sopranos and altos to countertenors. Then we'll only need to arrange a part of the score."

From then on, everyone got very busy. It is painstaking work to use the notes on a single piano to match people's keys. I was responsible for checking our practices and making sure that the vocals sounded right as our score gradually progressed, going back and forth between Engel and the rehearsal room. It had probably been the busiest time in my life. Three of our violin students and five choir students came to practice one day, saying they wanted to be a part of the performance. They were very welcome to join, but we didn't have the time to train them. It was all I could do to have them take some of the easier parts.

Engel yelled at one of the local violin students.

"No! You're off-key! Go back to the beginning again." The student tried harder.

"No, no! How many times must I repeat myself? Orvis in the second row, we're not using the original score. Take a good look at the score in front of you and try again. Taro, your fa is off again. Soichiro, don't laugh. Taro, try that fa again. Soichiro, try to get your ti a little higher. No, no, you're too slow. It starts like this."

Waving his baton furiously, Engel's intense training continued. It was the same with Janssen's rehearsals. An all-out effort was made and finally, the big day arrived. The final cultural exchange was to take place one day before the prisoners were *freed.*

The people of Bando performed a local dance called **Awa odori,** *where kimo-no-clad dancers moved with gusto to a very lively accompaniment.* The Otoko-odori *performed by the male dancers was lively and humorous, men in comical* hyottoko *masks painted with skewed features and puckered mouths, and variations of a local* Yakko-dako *dance had also been worked into the performance. The women were just as powerful and in no way resembled the gentle movements of traditional Japanese dances. As they kicked up their legs, glimpses of their white ankles flashed beneath their kimonos, giving cheering spectators a taste of healthy excitement.*

Everyone took part in the finale of the Awa odori. Manager Matsue, the Japanese soldiers, and the German soldiers all jumped into the crowd of dancers and found that the moves were not as easy as they had appeared. You don't look poised if your arms and legs don't move in sync or if your hips aren't planted firmly to support your body weight.

I was catching my breath when one of my peers called out to me. "Klaus! We're on! Let's give everyone one hell of a performance!" I gave him a thumbs-up.

The lower opening notes of the first movement sounded a little stiff, probably due to the tension among the musicians, but they seemed to loosen up in the second movement. It was as if they were beginning to let themselves go. As the music continued, the harmony began to capture everyone's heart. Our Japanese students joined the chorus climax. We began hearing voices from the people in the audience as well. I saw an old man raising a fist in the military-style and waving it back and forth in time to the music. I didn't realize that tears were falling from my eyes until the audience became a blur, but I wasn't embarrassed.

It wasn't just me. Engel and Hansen were crying, too. So was everyone else. We had truly understood the meaning of this piece.

The performance ended, and thunderous applause ensued. We ran down the makeshift scaffolding and embraced our friends, the residents of the community of Bando. Everyone was overwhelmed and in tears.

We were liberated the next day. We had a final roll call, then formed two lines and started walking toward the gate. The tears welled up again.

Engel's students were lined up just outside the gate. They were playing **Auld Lang Syne**. *Standing behind them were all the other locals, too many to count, waving tiny flags of Japan and Germany.*

We stopped and listened to the song, then shook hands with the local musicians and embraced Matsue and everyone else at the facility. Then I forced myself to put one foot in front of the other to proceed and began to sing Trout. My compatriots also began to sing. It was almost drowned out by the warm words of farewell that were coming from the residents. I took off my hat and threw it into the sky. The white hat soared high into the blue sky. The same burning sun that had scorched us on the day of our arrival was still there, shining brilliantly against my hat.

8

"I don't believe it!" Hannah, Arles, Rosa, and Edie said at the same time. Arles asked Klaus what types of pieces Klaus and the prison orchestra had played at Bando. Klaus reached into a pocket of his worn-out jacket and pulled out a piece of paper.

"I've always carried this around with me. It's my good luck charm. See for yourself, but please be careful not to tear it."

Arles took the note from Klaus. The list began with Beethoven's Symphony No. 9, and it had to contain at least thirty titles.

"I can't believe the story you just told us, Klaus," she said. The other members agreed.   "But it's true."

Hannah was getting even more confused.

"But Mr. Berger, this Tokushima—Japan—and the Nazis are allies, aren't they? Japan isn't doing anything to help us. How can that be if they're such nice people?"

"There probably isn't a single Japanese citizen who can answer that. Besides, Bando was very special. It wasn't the same at the other concentration camps in Japan, so we couldn't really talk openly about our time there."

"I'd like to go there, Mr. Berger. Let's all leave this hell, and you could take us to the Far East."

"Yes, we'll live through this," Leo agreed. "And we'll go to Bando! We're witnesses of these heinous crimes, and we'll call for peace in Bando."

Leo's enthusiasm spread among the other members of the orchestra and the air seemed to be charged, not that anyone truly believed that they would be able to visit Bando. But they desperately needed something to cling to.

"You're absolutely right," Klaus said. "That's a special mission that only we can accomplish." He was glad to see that everyone's spirits seemed to be elevated. "We wouldn't be able to survive if we didn't have hope." Klaus was pleased that Bando has become a pilgrimage site for the members of his orchestra, something that would give them hope to go on.

"I often tell my musicians about my time at Bando. Though some of them make me wonder why they became interested in music in the first place, every time I tell my story, it's like they're struck by a lightning bolt. Bando changed everything for me. When people appreciate music at the purest level, they can go beyond borders and languages, and even wars. It's much more gratifying than playing a Stradivarius or a Guarnerius, and I think that the ability to create music may be the single most important capacity that God has given us. Civilization can't enrich our emotions, and civilization can't eradicate wars, but I think culture is something that can fortify us so we can eliminate wars."

"But Klaus? Do you really think the Asian people understood our western music?"

"Arles, anyone can appreciate fine music. People are the same wherever you go; they'll look at a ruby and think it beautiful, whichever continent you may be in. And it isn't popular music that we're playing. We're playing true classics that have been enjoyed over a long period of time. The west isn't the only one who appreciate its beauty and clear texture; it can touch people's hearts anyplace in the world. It's the same as the sun that shines on everyone."

Klaus took a sip of his whisky. His cheeks became blushed as he continued to speak. "As a soloist, I used to be in fierce competition against others. It was in Bando that I understand the true beauty of music. I realized that it gave me the ability to promote true exchange that goes beyond language and culture. I have my cello, and the guitar that Dan taught me to play, and they gave me the courage to come here to Auschwitz."

Arles nodded in understanding.

"We've miraculously managed to stay alive because we have the most powerful weapons that exist."

"All right, I think we've talked enough. All of you, please remember this: for now, just focus on yourselves. Do it for your own survival and nothing else. Ensconce yourselves in your music. For the sake of your sanity, don't try to make a connection between your music and your present environment. This ridiculous situation can't go on forever. The things we've seen and done here will definitely be useful when we leave this place."

"You're right," Arles said. "We must close our hearts for now but keep our eyes wide open and watch everything. We owe it to everyone that was murdered here."

Chapter 4: Klaus and Hannah

1

The same routine continued in the days that followed. In the mornings, the orchestra would play for the prisoners as they left for work, and then they would head on to the train station to perform for one new arrival after another. They played waltzes in the afternoons to drown out the screams that came from the crematoriums, and were busy in the evenings with performances for the SS soldiers or the kapos, or writing scores or rehearsing.

Things were easier when they were busy. There was no time to stop and reflect, and their moves became mechanical. As the days went by, Rosa, Hannah, and anyone else who used to cry a lot became better at moving from one day to the next.

One day, Arles walked over to the medical block to see Marie. She should have recovered from her typhus by then, and Arles was looking forward to performing with her again. But the hospital room was empty except for the soiled sheets that remained on the beds. "No!"

Arles was shouting Marie's name when a woman stepped into the room. It was the female doctor with whom she had entrusted the younger woman's care. Arles ran to her and grabbed her by the collar of her white coat.

"Doctor, where's Marie? What happened to her?"

The doctor took a step back. She had only come back to make sure that the room had been cleared out.

"Marie? Oh, the violin player. She's recovered. But the chief doctor decided to send everyone to the gas chamber. She's probably being transported as we speak."

Arles went pale. She released her hold on the doctor's coat and ran out of the room. She made her way to the back door and saw a huge group of women being forced to board the rear of several trucks. They looked ill and were all naked. Though they weren't told where they were headed, utter despair filled their eyes. They were resigned to the fate that awaited them.

"Marie! Where are you? Marie!"

One of the women turned around. She had just reached for the handrail on one of the trucks and was about to pull herself up. She was beyond recognition. Her hair had grown in the short while that she had been hospitalized, plastered to her face by tears. She let go of the handrail and a kapo pushed her back up by her skeletal buttocks.

"Wait! She's healthy!" Arles ran to her and pushed the kapo with all her might, then turned around and faced the male doctor who was watching the proceedings.

"Doctor, what do you think you're doing? Let her come back! If you don't, I swear I will never, ever play another tune for you again. Are you happy with that? No? Give her back to me."

Trembling in her naked state, Marie clung to Arles and cried.

"Lucky bitch."

That was all the doctor said before he turned around and walked away. Marie understood that her life had just been spared. The other women were watching. Many began to cry harder. Arles put an arm around Marie's shoulder and turned the other way. She held Marie up and ran as fast as she could. Though she knew it was hard for Marie to run in her frail state, it was the only way to detach herself from the cries for help and the bitter resentment that she knew was pouring out of her doomed compatriots.

2

Arles heard the sound of music and turned her head. It was the male orchestra. They were playing *Kaiser Franz Joseph I, Rettungs-Jubel-Marsch* by Johann Strauss II. The purpose was to drown out the desperate cries that were coming from the trucks that were rumbling toward the gas chambers. Even trumpeters had been brought in to join the performance.

Arles released her hold on Marie and made her sit on the ground, then ran over to the conductor. Despite the enormous volume of the music, the orchestra was farther away than she had thought. Still, she continued to run as fast as she could, taking off her shoes along the way and screaming at the top of her lungs.

Klaus heard her screams. He had Leo take over the conducting and rushed toward her.   "What's the—"

"Stop it! Stop the music!" She tripped and fell to the ground. She grabbed a fistful of dirt and collapsed in tears. "Don't play a piece like that, please..."

"You're always so level-headed, Arles... what has made you so upset?" Arles sat on her knees and hit Klaus's chest with her dusty hands.

"I left them to die! There might have been a way to save them...but there was nothing that I could think of..." She broke down and wept.

Klaus looked up and saw Marie in the bushes a few yards away. She was curled up, naked, trembling, and crying, and he immediately understood what had just happened. He turned to his orchestra and raised his left hand to indicate that the performance is to be stopped. How much pain had Arles been holding back behind the fierce wall that she had encased her in? He could almost hear the wall shattering to pieces. He put his arms around her and held her tight. He removed his jacket. "Give this to Marie."

The horrid event was beyond anyone's worst nightmare. A total of seven thousand female patients had been squeezed into two barracks, where they spent two weeks crying and losing their sanity while waiting to be sent to the gas chambers. The trip to the gas chambers took two whole days from morning until late at night. The roaring sounds of the trucks and the desperate cries for help filled the sky along with the smoke that rose over Auschwitz.

From that day on, Arles became even more immersed in her music. She worked all day and spent all her nights looking for scores or writing arrangements, going without sleep for days on end. It was as if something had possessed her. She was fiercely determined and relentless, worse than the way she had been before Hannah arrived at Auschwitz, and forced her players to go over and over their parts until she was satisfied. Her heart was deeply wounded, and her eyes void of emotions. She was lost in her world of music, unable to tell what was real and what was not.

One morning, Arles did not show up for practice. Hannah went to her room and found her in bed with a fever. Hannah called the others and they rushed her to the medical wing.

Arles never regained her consciousness before she died. Arles had been respected by the SS soldiers. She had never yielded to the Nazis, and she had been empowered by her music. She may have been a prisoner, but had lived with a true sense of dignity.

"Can we tie this to the baton?" Marie asked. She was holding a faded, crumpled piece of fabric in the palm of her hand. It had been a hair ribbon that she had secretly maintained in her possession. It was all that she could think of doing for Arles at this point.

Everyone knew that Arles had been tough on Marie. She had once risked her life to save her, and though they were aware that she did not dislike her, she had seemed particularly critical of the younger woman. But Marie harbored no ill feelings. She was well aware that there had been a reason for Arles to pressure her. She would be on her way to the gas chamber again if her violin skills didn't quickly improve. Marie solemnly tied the mourning ribbon around the conductor's baton that Arles Bizet had always used.

3

From that day onward, Klaus merged the orchestras and became in charge of both. One day, no train arrived at the camp. No more smoke rose from the crematoria. People were beginning to sense that some kind of change was happening outside the camp. The orchestra members were ordered to dress in their formal wear and prepare to perform. They were led to the courtyard at one of the crematoria and found that a group of prisoners was assembled. They were the people who had been forced to work at the crematoria for many years, pushing their fellow prisoners into the gas chambers, then shaving the hair off the corpses, pulling out their gold teeth, and throwing them into the incinerator. Now it was their turn. They had to be silenced. They knew that this was the last time that they would get to hear music.

After the orchestra finished the hour-long performance, the prisoner number B54678, the representative of the group, stepped forward to shake hands with Klaus and the other musicians. The rest of the group followed. They were sobbing, but the corners of their mouths curved into slight smiles when they shook hands with the musicians in a final farewell. Knowing that they were about to head to their execution, Klaus did not have a word to say.

"Mr. Berger, and all of you fine musicians, thank you for your wonderful music. Your performances helped distract us from the things we had to do." The representative reached into his pocket and pulled out a few small items. "It makes no sense for us to hang on to these now. Please take them before the SS soldiers come back."

The precious goods had been taken from the corpses of their fellow prisoners. While Klaus was uncomfortable about accepting such things, it didn't seem right to decline what was clearly an expression of desperate gratitude from the last group of men to head for the gas chambers. Overwhelming emotions filled his chest upon hearing that the music at least comforted them in some way.

Later that day, the manager of the Auschwitz facility stopped by the music room. He was drunk.

"Our mission has now ended. Let's hear some music."

The orchestra performed *Ave Maria*. Huge tears began to roll down the manager's cheeks, and he covered them with both hands.

So it is true. It's over, Klaus thought to himself. *Perhaps we weren't the only ones who had been waiting to be freed from this hell.*

The dismantling of Auschwitz began a short while later. One by one, the members of the orchestra were called to the administrative office. They were told of their new fate, from which point they became separated from their peers. By this time, the musicians had become more fearful not of being liberated but of losing the colleagues with whom they had developed close bonds under extreme conditions. They faced death and worked through the worst time imaginable, and now their ties were being brutally severed before they could figure out what was happening.

Klaus stormed into the manager's office.

"Where are you taking the members of my orchestra? What's the meaning of this, suddenly making them leave before we can even figure out that they're missing?"

"You have done well, Berger," the manager said quietly as he smoked a pipe. "I appreciate the hard work that you have done for the Nazi Party. You may return to Berlin tomorrow. My men will take you part of the way, though I am not sure of the state that the city is in—"

"I didn't do it for the Nazis. I'm the conductor. Let me see where my members are headed. I want you to let me stay until the final musician leaves, and I want you to tell me where each of them is going."

The manager shook his head. "That will not be possible. You are to leave early tomorrow morning. Until then, we will be responsible for you."

"What?"

His pipe planted between his lips, the manager tilted his chin to indicate to his men to take the conductor away.

"What is this? Let go of me!"

Two soldiers grabbed Klaus under his arms and took him away. He was placed in a solitary cell.

The next morning, a huge black car was waiting for him. It was the same car that had driven him to Auschwitz. The manager and the SS soldiers watched as Klaus was driven out the gates, pained with worry about the fates of his fellow musicians.

4

The German soldiers were disbanded, and parts of the facilities were dismantled in order to destroy evidence of the mass killings. Edie, Marie, Rosa, and some of the others were sent somewhere else. Leo and Hannah were relocated to the Bergen-Belsen concentration camp in northern Germany. Auschwitz was a civilized place compared to Bergen-Belsen. No food was available, no medical room existed, and there were no roofs for the barracks. Prisoners were forced to endure the cold rain, which was also the only source of drinking water that they had. There were no crematoriums, and the dead were left lying on the ground. It was no exaggeration to say that Bergen-Belsen was probably the closest place to hell. Many of them died of dehydration or starvation, unaware that they would have been liberated in just a few days.

Hannah was drifting in and out of consciousness. She was looking for Leo in her mind as the memories slowly began to fade away. An image came to her mind of the silly tactics of love she and her sister once giggled about. Though

Auschwitz was far removed from the luxurious palaces the girls used to dream about, it was the place where Hannah had to quickly grow up. *Violin Concerto No. 3* echoed in her head.

Thoughts came and went: the satisfying feeling of playing music, the joy of leading the violin section as concertmaster, the things she used to enjoy as an ordinary girl—and then the images would blend into a hazy fog. She would regain consciousness for a moment, then slip into her dreams again. The strange thing was, it wasn't her parents nor other members of her family who kept appearing in her dreams.

Leo.

Suddenly, she heard voices. "Anyone still alive?"

"Hello?"

Male voices. There were several of them. The voices were breaking through her fog and coming closer. And closer. Her eyes fluttered open. She didn't have the strength to move a finger.

They've finally come to kill me.

Hannah was no longer afraid. She just wanted everything to end, and hoped they'd finish her off soon. No sound would come out of her mouth; her throat was completely parched. The only function that remained in her body was the slight movement of her eyes.

She then realized that the voices she was hearing were not speaking German.

Someone has finally come to rescue me? She was numb. She didn't have the strength to smile.

One of the men noticed her eyes move.

"We got one!"

He cradled Hannah in his arms and tried to pour water into her mouth. The water spilled down her chin as she didn't have the strength to swallow. But the icy sensation of the water made Hannah feel that she had been brought back to life. The man gently pressed her lips together and gave her water through his own mouth. He had repeated the action three times when Hannah's dazed eyes saw the British helmet that he was wearing.

"My God..."

A single tear fell down her cheek. The soldier cried out in joy. "You're going to make it! You're going to make it!" He supported her back with his knee, slowly pulled her up to a sitting position, and gave her water from his canteen. Hannah took some sips. The sudden intake of fluids made her cough, which seemed to bring some color back on her pale face. She was saved.

The soldier lifted her. The next thing she knew, she was lying in a hospital bed and an intravenous tube was connected to her arm.

5

"You're free now," said an American doctor. Hannah didn't understand English but his gestures were enough to reassure her. Although she was relieved to be alive, she was hit with an overwhelming sense of grief. Her mother was gone, her father was gone, and she had no idea what had happened to her little brother and her grandparents. She was alone. Hannah burst into tears in her hospital bed. How could she possibly go on?

"What's your name?" the doctor asked. She guessed correctly what the doctor was asking.

"Hannah. Hannah Janssen. Do you know Klaus—Klaus Berger?"

The doctor smiled as he wrote something on a pad and left her bedside.

It was a couple of days later that Klaus Berger and his wife came to see Hannah. Mrs. Berger saw her emaciated state and broke down in tears.

"Poor girl! Oh, Hannah, my husband told me everything. You've been so brave, I'm so glad you managed to pull through it all."

Mrs. Berger came to see her every day. Hannah went to live with the Bergers when she was strong enough to eat her meals again, but once she arrived at the house, she was overwhelmed by the memories. She found Andrew's tiny violin and ran out of the door. She covered her ears and screamed at the sound of music. She never even thought about opening her violin case when it was delivered. It was clear that she was very severely traumatized.

Mrs. Berger changed the carpets and the drapes, the layout of the furniture, and everything else that Hannah would see. But she would freeze at the entrance, frantically dig her fingernails into her scalp, and scream.

"The bad people are coming again. They're coming for me," she would mumble in confusion.

"No, Hannah, they aren't." That was all Mrs. Berger could say. All she could do was hold the girl in her arms and rock her gently as she continued to tremble. Klaus took over from his wife and tried to reassure Hannah that she was safe.

"Listen to me, Hannah. No one's coming for you. The was is over."

He rented a second-floor apartment for Hannah, thinking that a change of scenery might do her good. It was located close to their house, and he and his wife put up pink curtains and arranged the décor in warm, bright colors. They set Hannah's violin case in a corner by the door. It was the start of her new life.

Mrs. Berger tried to get Hannah into a normal routine and took her shopping one day. But as the music flowed from the store, Hannah's face gradually became pale. She felt dizzy, vomited, and collapsed. Mrs. Berger took her to see a psychiatrist. The doctor invited them into his examination room. He told Mrs. Berger to sit in a chair at the end of the room and watch his exchange with the patient, hoping that she could pick up Hannah's conditions objectively. He examined Hannah and placed a phonograph in front of her.

"From what Mrs. Berger has told me, Hannah, I think you have an acute fear of sounds. You've been through terrible ordeals and now suddenly been relieved of the constant tension, which I think has had a huge impact on your autonomic nervous system. But I have good news for you. I believe time will heal, and you'll come back to being yourself. I'm going to play some records now so we can identify the types of sounds that make you uncomfortable. Raise your right hand if you start to feel uncomfortable."

The doctor played some sounds. First, it was birds chirping, followed by the smooth sounds of a flowing river, then the rumbling of a car engine. Hannah raised her hand. She started to be queasy.

Next came the sound of children playing, then *Voices of Spring* by Johann Strauss II. Hannah covered her ears and screamed. She stood up, ran over to Mrs. Berger, and buried her face in her knees, and cried. Mrs. Berger shook her head. Her lips trembled as she held Hannah and gently ran her fingers through her hair.

"Doctor, the agony that Hannah's been through has to be beyond our imagination. How can we Germans ever make it up to her and others like her?"

"It'll be very difficult, madam. We tend to look away from history, and in that sense, we're sick, too. Every one of us needs to open our eyes and try to better ourselves and make sure that nothing even remotely similar ever happens again, and I believe that we should be able to do that. But it isn't just us. If people throughout the world can learn from this, everyone will start to give more thought to peace. The human race is not stupid."

Mrs. Berger was not the only one who had been feeling guilty about the Holocaust. The doctor had also suffered from a guilty conscience.

"To do that, we mustn't turn away from the facts. We need to face what the Nazis did. The Jews and the Poles who come to me don't want to talk about it. We cannot make things better immediately. I know it will take a long time. The only thing that I can do now is to treat my patients like Hannah."

Mrs. Berger nodded. Tears were running down her cheeks as she tightened her hold on Hannah.

"You're right, doctor. And we're going to make Hannah better."

6

It wasn't easy. The days went by without a clue as to how Hannah's condition could be improved. Her windows remained closed, her curtains were drawn, and she would stay locked up in her room all day, shutting out all sounds. Mrs. Berger brought her meals each day, and she would read magazines she brought along that had nothing to do with the genocide. She put earplugs in Hannah's ears on her visits to the doctor, where he would chat with her about some nonchalant things.

Two months went by. She was finally beginning to improve. There was a sparkle in her eyes one day when Mrs. Berger came to the apartment with her meal.

"I've noticed a very nice smell in the morning," she said.

"Oh, it must be the bakery across the street, they sell freshly baked bread. Would you like to go there tomorrow morning?" There were tears in Mrs. Berger's eyes as she watched Hannah speaking animatedly, and she called the doctor as soon as she got home.

"I see," he said. "Perhaps Hannah has finally started to open up. Take her to the bakery tomorrow. But please make sure to have her wear her earplugs, just to be on the safe side."

Mrs. Berger could sense that the doctor was excited about the progress as well. "Right. I'll let you know how it goes."

Hannah and Mrs. Berger went to the bakery early the next morning. Located just across the street, the shop was filled with the delicious aromas of baked bread, butter, and the sweet scents of jams. A tall baker brought a tray out of the oven and wrapped a butter roll in paper and handed it to Hannah.

"Try this, young lady. Careful, it's hot."

"This smells heavenly. I didn't know that bread could be so hot and so soft." She took a bite. "Delicious! Mrs. Berger? Can I get five of these?"

"We can get as many as you like, Hannah. I'd like five rolls, too."

"Here you go, ten altogether," the baker said as he put the oven-fresh rolls in two paper bags. "Come back soon, sweetie."

"Thank you," Hannah said with a big smile on her face.

They returned to the apartment without incident, and Mrs. Berger walked over to the window and opened it a fraction, drawing the curtains open and neatly tying their ends to let the sun in.

"Come here, Hannah. You can smell the bread from across the street. You'll be able to enjoy these wonderful aromas every morning."

Hannah cautiously walked over to the window and inhaled. The soft spring breeze carried in the warm scent of buttery, toasted bread. From that day, Hannah started to open her window at eight o'clock every morning.

One day, she was eating a butter roll and glancing out her partially open window when a white dove flew over and planted itself on her windowsill. It looked at her and crooned.
Hannah tore off a tiny morsel and placed it on the palm of her hand. The dove stretched its neck, pecked it, and then took off.

It came back at the same time the next day and every morning after that. Hannah named the dove "Kluck".

"Come back again tomorrow, Kluck. I'll be waiting for you with more bread."

Kluck provided an opportunity for Hannah to open the door to her heart a little more each day. The dove also made her feel better about the sounds of car engines and gave her a reason to get out of the apartment. Before long, she was able to go to the bakery on her own, even without the earplugs.

Mrs. Berger called the doctor and reported to him the good news.

"Doctor, Hannah has a new friend, a dove that comes to see her every day, and she goes to the bakery each morning so she can buy bread to feed it."

"That's excellent, Mrs. Berger. But we'll need to continue to watch her carefully."

Hannah was still unable to tolerate the sound of music. She would cover her ears when she heard a record being played and crouch in the middle of the street.

It was Hannah's idea, however, to one day go to a concert, thinking that shock therapy might be what she needed.

The doctor disagreed. "There's no need to rush things. Something will come your way, like that dove at your window." But Hannah was adamant. She sat in the last row at the concert hall so she wouldn't have a good view of the orchestra.

It began to perform Mozart's *Eine Kleine Nachtmusik*. Though she was wearing earplugs, Hannah could make out what they were playing from the muffled sounds that made their way through the gaps in the earplugs. In her eyes, the conductor was cast in sepia color, as if the performance was taking place in another world.

The second performance was Bach's *Air on the G String*. It had been her mother's favorite. Hannah loosened her earplugs, and the sound of the music came closer. Tears began to roll down her cheeks. But she continued to listen. She did not panic. She closed her eyes and took in the melody.

Though she didn't dare to remove her earplugs, Hannah reminisced about happier days. She thought about Andrew and her grandfather. There had not been a single word about them. She assumed they were most likely gone. She was also aware that the Burgers probably knew as well but were avoiding the subject. She just couldn't bring herself up to confirm with anyone what she knew in her heart.

That was when the plug on her left ear fell out. Suddenly, the orchestra started to play *Radetzky March*. It was very loud. Too loud. Hannah covered her ears and screamed. And she collapsed on the spot. The sudden incident caused a stir in the audience and led to a suspension of the concert. An ambulance was called and Mr. and Mrs. Berger, along with her doctor, rushed over to the hospital. She was given a strong sedative and was asleep when they arrived.

7

Once again, Hannah closed her windows and always kept them locked. She didn't see her doctor, and no longer visited the bakery shop. She stopped brushing her hair and stayed in her pajamas. She was like a sleepwalker, wandering around her tiny apartment all day and all night. She even closed herself off from Mrs. Berger. The older woman was full of concern, but it was all she could do to bring Hannah her meals. Hannah had locked herself up in her own world.

"She's only going to get worse, madam," the doctor said to Mrs. Berger one day, handing her a finely ground psychotropic drug.

"Put this in her lunch tomorrow. Wait an hour, go inside her apartment, and wait for me to arrive."

"All right, doctor. I'll do that."

The medication worked. Hannah was sound asleep in her bed when Mrs. Berger stepped in. She quietly greeted the doctor as he walked in with his phonograph. She watched nervously as he went to Hannah and played a recording of *Air on the G String*.

A single tear fell from the corner of Hannah's eye.

The doctor sat close to her and watched her every little movement. He quietly greeted her. Hannah's eyes remained closed as she began to speak.

"I'm sorry, doctor. I don't know how I can go on living. I should have died back there with everyone else."

"Oh, Hannah…" Mrs. Berger pressed her eyes with a handkerchief.

"I understand, Hannah, I really do," the doctor said in a soft voice. He stroked her shoulder in a gentle, soothing manner and continued to speak. "But listen to me, you aren't alone. You've been given a chance to live, and there are things that you still need to do."

The effects of the medication made his voice sound to Hannah as if it were coming from a faraway place.

"Get some rest, sweetheart, and we'll all go back to Auschwitz tomorrow. That's the place where you've left your heart. We'll go back there and take a good look at the place. It will help us find a way for you to go on."

"…I'm scared…"

"I know you are, honey." Mrs. Berger said, gently stroking her hair. "We'll be there with you."

Another tear rolled down. She slowly nodded; eyes still closed.

The next morning, Hannah woke up feeling rested. It had been a while since she last slept so well. Mrs. Berger had removed the curtains during her visit the previous day, and Hannah had been awakened by the bright sunlight that poured.

Didn't someone mention Auschwitz? Hannah wasn't sure where the idea had come from, but for some reason, she wasn't afraid. In fact, she knew she needed to go back there.

The Bergers came to the apartment a short while later.

"Mrs. Berger, I—I seem to have fallen asleep. I think I had a dream. Someone— I don't know who it was, but someone… was saying we would go to Auschwitz…it's as if my mother was calling me back…"

"Yes, Hannah, we'll all go together."

"Bring your violin," Klaus said. "Carry it on your back, the same way you did when you first arrived there."

8

Hannah was soon back at Auschwitz. This time, with Mr. and Mrs. Berger and her doctor. The sign that read "Work Brings Freedom" was still up at the gate and standing proudly under the sun, as well as a part of the stone blocks that remained intact. The railroad tracks were no longer in use and rusted, covered with weeds. The road that hundreds of thousands of people had traversed for forced labor no longer remained and the desolate earth was now covered with a colorful array of poppies that were swaying in the early summer breeze. There was no more smoke to turn the sky a dull gray. Instead, white clouds were floating in the blue sky. Only the chimneys that had incinerated countless victims were still there, abandoned and piercing the sky.

Hannah was unable to move. She stood there and stared. She couldn't remember how the place was while she was imprisoned there. Had there been a field of poppies back then? It had been such a struggle just to survive, she realized now that she had never had the time to look around the surroundings. She recalled the black and brown barracks, the filthy prison uniforms people were forced to wear, the gloomy, smoke-filled sky…No, she didn't think there had been brightly colored flowers in this place.

Then who planted them?

For some reason, Hannah felt a bit less tense. She was surprised to find that the deep sadness and rage were dissipating.

Klaus walked into the field of poppies and found a big rock from where he had a good view of the gate. He sat on the rock and pulled out his cello. Quietly, he began to play *Ave Maria*. He started singing and glanced at Hannah, gesturing her to join him. That was when the realization hit her. The amazing field of blooming poppies had to be the spirits of the thousands of people who had perished there. It was her mother, her father, her grandfather, and Andrew. They were all here with the poppies, and they were cheering her on.

I didn't want you to leave me. I didn't want you to die.

Maybe it was her duty now to comfort their soul and all the other people who died there so their spirits could go to heaven. She had spent time here with Arles, the proud and gifted musician. This was where Klaus had told her about the miracle in Bando. There was Hans, the bloodthirsty murderer who had shed tears when he listened to her *Ave Maria*. There was Edie, Marie, Rosa—and Leo. Their images popped into her mind as if she were looking through a kaleidoscope. She had survived, and she was standing here at Auschwitz again, filled with a deep sense of gratitude for being able to come back.

There is still something that I must do here.

She pulled out her violin and walked over to where Klaus was playing his cello. She played *Ave Maria* with him.

Mrs. Berger could not stop her tears. "Doctor, look…she's playing her violin again."

He smiled. "The treatment is over now. We, too, have just defeated the Nazis."

9

Hannah and Klaus, along with Mrs. Berger, soon relocated and began to visit the field of poppies every day, always at dusk—the same hour that they used to perform for the people returning after their forced labor—and played *Ave Maria*. The wind sometimes carried the melody afar to be heard at people's homes some distance away.

Years went by, and more people began to talk about their performances. Another surviving member of the orchestra joined, and then another. Ten former members were eventually performing amid the poppies. Edie and Leo were among them.

Leo had been rescued by the British soldiers and relocated to America, the land of freedom, and changed his name in an attempt to forget the ordeal. The *Ave Maria* performance by the ten musicians caught the attention of the visitors. News began to spread about the musicians who had survived the Holocaust, and they started receiving requests to perform at other venues.

Hannah was saved by Leo yet again. They realized that they had been in love with each other the whole time, and together they began to heal through their music. Hannah always played Pugnani's *Largo Espressivo* at the end of the performances, recalling bittersweet memories of the family she had once had.

The seasons had come and gone. The poppies were once again in full bloom. One day, after their performance of *Ave Maria*, Hannah did not start *Largo Espressivo*. Leo turned to her. "Hannah?" Hannah was seated in her small chair, her violin clutched between her shoulder and her chin. She didn't move. There was a satisfied smile on her face as if she had fulfilled a mission from heaven. She was able to deliver requiems for all the people who had perished at Auschwitz.

"Hannah! You haven't played *Largo* yet! We promised we'd all go to Bando together!" Leo's eyes were filled with tears as he gently pulled the violin off her shoulder.

The violin that Hannah had played each day became what people called the Ave Maria Violin. Leo donated it to a museum.

Chapter 5: Mr. Calsas and Leo

1

"And that's the whole story about the Ave Maria Violin," Mr. Calsas said. He finished talking as if he had just completed a big mission or something.

Mr. Kiyohara and I were stunned. For a while there, neither of us could utter a word. It wasn't as if I had been expecting a fun story behind this violin, but this was really heavy stuff.

"Oh!" Mr. Kiyohara suddenly exclaimed. He pulled out his penlight and pointed it inside the F-hole in the Ave Maria Violin. The light didn't reach far inside the instrument.

"If everything you've told us is true, then I think Hannah's mother's letter should still be inside."

He borrowed a thin, long piece of wire from the staff and angled it inside like he was fishing, and there it was—the letter that had been written by Hannah's mother. It looked like there were tear stains smudged on the back. We could see bloodstains on the front that appeared to show fingerprints—Hannah's mother's fingerprints—that were stuck onto the paper in a blackish-red color. The paper was weathered with age and looked like it was about to be torn into pieces, so we decided not to unfold it. Mr. Kiyohara handled it very, very carefully and said we should donate it to the Auschwitz Museum. There would be no more double echoes coming out of this violin.

I looked at Mr. Calsas and asked him. "Hannah and Leo loved each other, right? Why didn't they get married?"

"Yes, Asuka, they were very much in love. I think someday when you're older, you'll probably understand that a bond of love can sometimes be made deeper through music, so much deeper than a ceremony," he said, smiling. "The American poet Walt Whitman once described the Japanese people as 'the children of Brahma'. These are noble, dignified people who have a beautiful spirit that's filled with courage and goodwill. I think music is a gift from God that will save us from evil and allow us to become divine in spirit. I once saw children performing the violin at Carnegie Hall, and they were taught by a Japanese teacher and his German wife. The couple has been inspiring hundreds of thousands of Brahman children throughout the world. It's interesting that on one hand, a German named Hitler created hell on earth while this German lady and her Japanese husband are out there creating Brahman children.

Even today, ethnic conflicts and acts of terror continue to occur, and new forms of hell are being created in different parts of the globe. I believe that when we're able to have those thoughtless people pick up musical instruments in the place of guns and they start to open up and share each other's culture, their children will become Brahman subjects and our world will finally achieve true peace."

"But Mr. Calsas, how could we make something like that happen?"

"That's a tough question to answer. What do you think?"

I tried to gather up the little knowledge that I have in my brain and did my best to come up with an answer.

"What if bands or orchestras went in and attacked war zones? What if the soldiers came out of their tanks and suddenly started playing musical instruments instead of firing cannons? They would do it every day, and they would even play the ethnic music of the enemy. Or how about surrounding the enemy with music and brainwashing them into believing that they can't live without music? Then maybe they wouldn't want to fight wars anymore."

"Those are pretty interesting ideas that you have, Asuka. Advances in civilization won't save the world, but culture just might. It all depends on people's mindsets."

Mr. Kiyohara smiled. "It's important that we have music, food, work, and education on peace. Concentrate on your practices, Asuka. Think of Hannah."

"Hey, Mr. Calsas, I have an idea. Let's take this violin and go to Bando."

I knew I was getting off-topic, but Bando, the place that Mr. Calsas said Klaus Berger had lived as a POW, was not too far away from where I lived. There is no camp anymore, but I thought it might be nice to take Hannah's violin there for her. Mr. Calsas seemed to like the idea. It was like fate was bringing us together—Hannah's violin and me, a girl from Tokushima. He promised he'd try to bring all the survivors of the Berger orchestra to Bando around the time the poppies were in bloom.

Mr. Kiyohara turned to Mr. Calsas. "But sir, may I ask you how you know so much about Hannah? Were you there too…?"

"You'll find out soon enough," the old man said, and it didn't seem right for us to press on with more questions.

2

Mr. Calsas told us that he was going back to rehearsal, so we said good-bye and started heading home to Tokushima. It isn't like I'm about to die, and I know that my life will continue to be peaceful tomorrow and the day after that. I don't think I will die from skipping practice, either. But if I'm too lazy to practice and keep putting it off every day, I'll never be anywhere nearly as good as Hannah had been. It would be meaningless for me to have this violin.

"It's Hannah's precious violin that you have there, Asuka," my mother said, breaking my thoughts. "You need to do justice, you know. You'll need to practice harder."

"Will you be quiet, Mom? I'm trying to think."

I know I was brusque. I was thinking of different things without being able to come up with the answers. I was concentrating on my thoughts, and it sounded like Mom was about to start another one of her lectures. Normally, we would have gotten into an argument. But I realized then that nothing was going to change if I kept having arguments with my mom. I apologized.

"Sorry. I know it's important to practice, but I was thinking about what Mr. Calsas told us today. I know you have things you want to say to me, but I can't think and answer at the same time…so can I think things through for a minute?"

"Of course, Asuka. I'm sorry if it sounded like I was trying to lecture you. I know you're old enough to think for yourself."

This was different. It was positive.

Mr. Kiyohara, who had been watching our exchange, raised his hand to indicate that he wanted to put in a word.

"Everyone has a mission, Asuka, and you own the Ave Maria Violin. The fact that this violin came to you instead of me might mean that you were given a special mission. I think you're going to end up being a fine child of Brahma."

I didn't argue. I nodded.

"Uh, Mom, I want to take lessons in Tokyo. I know you want me to become a doctor, but I want to do serious work with this violin."

"Okay, Asuka. I'll talk to your teacher so you can take lessons in Tokyo."

Mom wasn't against the idea. I'm sure she probably wasn't all that excited about it, but she sensed that I was serious this time.

Starting on that day, I stopped saying no to everything, even if it was something that I didn't want to do, and I tried to put others before me. I'm not sure if I really understand what it means to be living in a peaceful world and I can't explain it, but I think I've gotten a feel for it. As I was preoccupied with music, my grade for the midterm right after Osaka were terrible.

Surprisingly enough, my mother didn't get upset. She explained to me that, more than the grades on a single test, she now sees the importance of a seed that was planted which could eventually grow to something significant in my life. I think she is right. Though I flinched when I got my test back, my *Ave Maria* was starting to sound better and better. It probably wasn't technical. I had a feeling that hearing about Hannah was helping me to make beautiful music.

I used to think that my mother complained too much. I can see now that she wanted me to feel and experience different things and was just getting ahead of me. Though I've always been afraid to have her find out that I'm no genius, just an average girl, my mother was well aware and was okay with it. She's been doing her best to guide me on a path to become a doctor as a fallback plan. I realized that and thought happily that I could never outdo her. As they say, mother knows best.

3

"Asuka! I have wonderful news for you!"

It was almost the end of the school year. My mother had just gotten off the phone and came running into my room.

"What is it?"

"Mr. Kiyohara has an amazing offer. How would you like to go to Europe next summer?"

"Huh?"

"To perform at the Budapest Music Festival in Hungary, the Vienna Music Festival in Austria, the Salzburg Festival, and other music festivals in Germany!"

According to my mother, it started when Mr. Kiyohara contacted a radio station in Poland trying to find information about the Ave Maria Violin before we met Mr. Calsas. He told her that many people who listened to the show called the radio station saying they wanted to hear what this Ave Maria Violin sounded like, which eventually led to the offer.

"He said they've set up a plan to have kids from different countries take part, and they want you to be a part of it. They want you to play *Ave Maria*."

"You mean, solo?" I was stunned.

"Of course." Mom grinned happily and said her usual line. "You had better practice."

My lessons became tougher. The teacher was more demanding, and everything was carefully checked over and over—the emotiveness of the music, the expressions of the soul—and I tackled each of my issues as I imagined playing for an audience. The lessons went on, I persevered. Summer break finally arrived, and I flew to Europe.

Besides the two participants from Japan, there were about ten others from different countries, including the United States, Canada, UK, Australia, Germany, France, Switzerland, and China. Naturally, everyone spoke a different language. But because we had music, a common thread between us, it took us no time to become friends. We were speaking in our own language but somehow were able to communicate pretty well. Though there was barely any time for rehearsals, everything went great. The adults who were with us seemed to be astonished.

And finally, it was the day of our last performance. We were at St. Stephen's Cathedral in Austria. None of us were nervous as we'd already performed at all the other places, but this time, the venue was a cathedral and not the usual concert hall. We couldn't help getting a bit overwhelmed when we saw the majestic cathedral and the fabulous stained-glass windows. The clear echoes there would give away the tiniest mistakes that we made.

Though we'd been getting terrific turnouts everywhere we went, this performance was going to be something else. A huge crowd had gathered, and there were people who had to stand outside because there weren't enough seats for everyone inside. They decided to open the Giant Gate for the performance.

It began with Fiocco's *Allegro*, followed by Vivaldi's *Violin Concerto in A minor*, Boccherini's *Minuet*, Weber's *Chorus of Foresters*, Bach's *Minuet No. 2*, a unison of *Twinkle, Twinkle, Little Star*, Pachelbel's *Canon in D*, Japanese songs

Hamabe no Uta (Come Walk Along the Shore), and *Furusato (Hometown).* The audience roared in excitement and offered never-ending applause and stomped their feet when our group of performers stepped onto the stage. The bravos were finally beginning to settle down when the mayor of Vienna rose from his seat.

"Ladies and gentlemen, our last performance will feature the Ave Maria Violin. Being performed here today is, of course, *Ave Maria.*"

It looked like the whole audience got on their feet before the mayor could even finish talking. There was a thunder of applause, which is something I still couldn't get used to because people seem to expect so much that it gets really terrifying. I stood at the center of the stage, looked up at the stained-glass windows at the entrance, took a deep breath, and bowed.

That was when an old man with a cello and a middle-aged lady came walking toward me from stage right.

"Mr. Calsas?"

"Good to see you again, Asuka."

I was so surprised to see him that I forgot that I was standing in front of a huge audience and hugged him. We were like that for a few moments and then he picked up the microphone and turned back to the crowd.

"Ladies and gentlemen, I have an announcement. My name is Leo Rochester. I played *Ave Maria* with Hannah Janssen and this violin throughout our time at Auschwitz."

"What?"

I didn't understand English much but I got the gist of what he was saying. Did he say Leo? Mr. Calsas was Leo? I had to be the most stunned person in the cathedral. He looked at me as my mouth hung open, and winked.

"And this lady here is Sara Berger, the niece of Klaus Berger, the man who hid Hannah and her family in his home, then volunteered to go to Auschwitz to try to protect them and conducted the orchestra there. If we may, we would like to join in this performance."

Everyone in the audience was on their feet, clapping their hands in thunderous applause. There were tears in the mayor's eyes as he stepped onto the stage and welcomed Mr. Calsas and Ms. Berger. I didn't think the applause was ever going to end.

It eventually quietened down, and I took another bow. I held the Ave Maria Violin in position and could hear people in the audience holding their breath. The piano accompaniment began, and I started to play *Ave Maria*. The sound resonated more clearly inside the cathedral than at any other venue. The melody was soothing. It might be strange to say that I felt cleansed by the sounds that were coming from my own performance, but that's the way I felt. Everything else left my mind as I focused on playing the beautiful piece. The waves of sweet, clear music seemed to gently seep into the hearts of everyone in the audience.

Mr. Calsas joined in with his cello, and Sara's vocals came toward the end of the piece, their sounds so beautiful that they seemed ethereal. It was like a prayer for those who have gone far beyond the worst suffering imaginable. The melody seemed to reach out to God, asking him to protect and bring eternal peace to the many innocent lives that were so violently taken—and the people in the audience were in tears.

Our performance came to an end. No one moved. It was completely still. We held hands and gave a deep bow. Then suddenly, applause broke out from the people who were sitting in the front row as they jumped out of their seats. The people behind them followed suit. A huge wave of smiles and tears came rushing toward us. The performance had been a huge success.

Postlude: Hannah and Asuka

Our tour ended, and I went to Auschwitz with Sara and Mr. Calsas.

Wow.

That was all I could say.

Colorful poppies were in full bloom across the fields at what remains today of the Auschwitz—as I imagined it would have been decades ago when Hannah had first returned here to play her violin. There was no one around to watch us as the three of us performed *Ave Maria*.

There was something I wanted to do before we were on our way.

"I'd like to play that piece for Hannah—the piece she hadn't been able to play."

"You'd do that for her?"

"Yes, sir. For Hannah. And for you, Mr. Calsas...I mean Leo."

I did my best to explain what I wanted to do in my broken English. Tears welled up in Leo's eyes. As I had suspected, time seemed to have been suspended for him since that day, long ago, when Hannah suddenly stopped playing her violin. I didn't think Auschwitz would truly end for Mr. Calsas until he heard *Largo Espressivo* played on her violin.

I thought about Hannah and began to play.

A long time ago when I was young, I used to belong to our family
Mother with her gentle smiles
Father brusque but strong
Grandmother silently held me
Sweet, sweet grandfather

My beautiful sister with a mind that freed from her physical challenges
Little Andrew, who I wanted more time to play with
You were my precious family.
I was young
I thought happiness would last forever
If God would grant me just one wish
There's only one thing that I would ask
Once more time
Just one more time
I'd like to go back to the way we were.

I finished playing the piece and saw a pretty red poppy swaying in the breeze by our feet. I knew that it had to be Hannah.

The End